THE ISL

RICHARD PRICE has published over a dozen books of poetry since his debut in 1993, including *Lucky Day* (2005), which was a *Guardian* Book of the Year and shortlisted for the Whitbread Poetry Prize. In 2013 *Small World* won the Creative Scotland Award for the Best Poetry Collection of that year. It was followed by another *Guardian* Book of the Year, *Moon for Sale* (2017). *The Owner of the Sea* (2021), re-telling Inuit stories, was a *Scotsman* Book of the Year. More recent works include *Late Gifts*, a braided work which ties consumerism's interaction with the environment to a narrative of a middle-aged father and his son. For over thirty years he was a curator and then manager of curators at the British Library, before becoming a freelance writer in 2024. He is a tutor at the Poetry School, London.

Also by Richard Price

SHORT STORIES

A Boy in Summer

POETRY

Tube Shelter Perspective
Sense and a Minor Fever
Marks & Sparks
Hand Held
Perfumes and Petrol Fumes
Frosted, Melted
Lucky Day
Greenfields
Earliest Spring Yet
Lute Variations
Rays
Small World
Moon for Sale
The Owner of the Sea
Late Gifts

ARTISTS BOOKS

Gift horse with Ronald King
Release Every Pattern with Chan Ky-Yut
Little but often with Ronald King
Wake Up and Sleep with Caroline Isgar
Folded with Julie Johnstone
Sedna and the Fulmar with Ronald King
Digital with Julie Johnstone
Tinderness with Simon Lewandowski
Sweet apple with Julie Johnstone

ESSAYS

Is This A Poem?

THE ISLAND

RICHARD PRICE

SALT

CROMER

PUBLISHED BY SALT PUBLISHING 2026

2 4 6 8 10 9 7 5 3 1

First published in Great Britain in 2010 by
Two Ravens Press Ltd

This edition published in Great Britain in 2026 by
Salt Publishing Ltd
12 Norwich Road, Cromer NR27 0AX United Kingdom

GPSR representative
Matt Parsons matt.parsons@upi2mbooks.hr
UPI-2M PLUS d.o.o., Medulićeva 20, 1,0000 Zagreb, Croatia

www.saltpublishing.com

Salt Publishing Limited Reg. No. 5293401

A CIP catalogue record for this book is available from the British Library

ISBN 978 1 78463 403 2 (Paperback edition)
ISBN 978 1 78463 404 9 (Electronic edition)

Typeset in Neacademia by Salt Publishing

Printed and bound in Great Britain by Clays Ltd, Elcograf S.p.A

MIX
Paper | Supporting responsible forestry
FSC® C018072
www.fsc.org

THE ISLAND

1

LIONS AND TIGERS

"AWAY AND RECYCLE *yourself*, then," Linda Urquhart was shouting as Graham slammed the door behind him. He heard a picture fall off the wall inside: it could only be his mother's holiday painting, from years ago.

The bags in his hands clinked as he moved off, and Jas cocked her head. "Dad be a bit careful?" she said, mimicking a hundred warnings he'd given her in the past.

"Jasmine be *very* careful, OK!"

He was keeping his tone even. He was keeping his tone almost even.

Softer: "Because I can't hold your hand."

He lifted the bags to show her. "Stay on the inside of the pavement, alright?"

"I'd like to see tigers and lions today," she said, as if this was the natural answer to his request.

"We're only going to the bottle bank. We'll go to the Zoo another day."

Jas looked at the couple of plastic animals she was holding and gave the consoling echo, "We'll go to the Zoo another day."

He had control of the bottles.

Father and daughter walked on in silence.

Before long Jas started to skip a few paces ahead of him. She could do this in only one way, leading with her left foot. She was trying it with her right but was blocked by the thought of it. At the end of five irregular semi-hops she stumbled then recovered. They both laughed.

"That was a bit funny?" she said, looking up at him. There was a suggestion of doubt, but she looked him in the eye and laughed again, deliberately, confidently this time. She skipped ahead of him, strong left, weak right.

Bit, Graham thought: I need to work on vocabulary.

At the three-way junction she waited for him, and he put the bags down to lift her up. She pressed the button.

Through a superimposed sticker a nearly white word lit up: WAIT.

The sticker said Save The Trees Fight The Link.

"Come on Green Man!" Jas told the light on the traffic island.

The Red Man would not surrender his vigil.

Graham thought he might just walk her over in any case. Last time he had risked this, Jasmine had upbraided him, "That's naughty!"

He'd replied: "Grown ups can see danger from far away."

The Red Man conceded before Graham had made up his mind to cross.

Finally, after a few seconds, Green stepped visibly out of his tunnel's darkness, mimed assent.

Graham carried Jas and the bags awkwardly to the traffic island and set his daughter down.

They had to wait again.

This lane was busier. Graham clutched both bags with one hand and gripped Jas's hand firmly with the other. He pressed the traffic button himself.

"I don't like it!" she squealed, twisting out of his grip, letting slip one of the plastic figures, a tiger, on to the pavement and stepping into the road.

A yellow cabriolet with its top down was racing towards her, its driver with his head slightly bent. He was speaking rapidly into his phone, in thrall to his sentences. He was oblivious to the human detail on the road.

"I want to walk on my own!" Jas turned to say as Graham froze before her.

The car did not slow.

He was unable to call her name.

He was unable to call her name because he was deep inside a fraction of trying to call her name.

He was unable to call her name because he was far far outside a fraction of trying to call her name.

He heard "Jasmine!" in his head, felt it in his chest, heard it failing to be translated to his voice, failing to be translated to the action of his arms and fingers.

The car did not slow.

Graham lurched towards her.

At the same time Jas saw the miniature tiger she had dropped on the traffic island. She evaded her father's outstretched arms, stepped back into safety, and picked the toy up.

"Tie-Tie! Don't get lost!"

Graham jumped back with a jolt, the bottles clinking again, and the car swept by them.

The yellow car only slowed when it had passed them. The

driver turned his head away from his phone and shouted back at them: "Keep your fucking brat on a lead if you can't control it."

2

FIVE GREEN BOTTLES

GRAHAM TOOK HIS first new breaths as the yellow car accelerated again. Moving out of his line of view it sped round a louvred outhouse, an electrical substation or a bin park.

At the traffic lights on the other side of the road, the second Green Man illuminated.

"Come on Tie-Tie," Jas said to the tiger, "Don't be slow."

Graham took Jas's hand with a snatch as she started to walk ahead of him, still holding the two bags with his other hand, and they crossed the road together.

By the time they reached the bottle bank, sited in the middle of a supermarket car park, Graham's left arm was aching with the weight of the bottles. They'd crossed the path of several twitchy family cars, mothers looking for spaces. Jas was pulling at his side, trying to escape.

Graham could feel himself filmed in sweat.

"We're nearly there."

"Giant playboxes!" Jas said.

"Right," Graham said, "Marmite first."

Jas grabbed at the bags, "I want to do it! I want to do it!"

The exclamatory phase, Graham thought.

Jas picked up one of the jars, in her hands a small cauldron.

Graham lifted her up to the brown-coloured skip and she tried to push the jar through the stiff fibres guarding its opening. There was no give. The jar just slipped out of her hands and broke on the concrete at Graham's feet.

"Aw, never mind. Maybe I can help with the next one?"

"No! I want to do it!"

"Well you have to really push this time, OK?"

Jas really pushed this time, but the bristles were springy. They sent the jar in a failed parabola just past Graham's elbow, breaking on the kerb edge.

"Careful now!" a woman passer-by said, adding, "Cars do use this car-park you know!"

There was only one brown bottle left in the bag, the former home of liquid paracetamol. The medicine was rendered in a concentration suitable, it had been judged, for infants. Linda and Graham always kept a bottle spare.

This time Graham made sure to help Jas at the last moment. There was a brief protest, overwhelmed by a squeal – delight – as the bottle was heard smashing in the metal depths.

"Green ones now," he said.

He moved Jas over to the green skip. There were five green bottles and, as they destroyed them one by one, Graham began a version of the children's song. Jas soon joined in and they finished with "No green bottles sitting on the skip."

All that were left in the bags were three clear jam jars and an empty wine bottle made from blue glass.

They moved to the white skip.

It was a strain lifting her up like this.

"Another song!"

"Aw, you don't want to do it again do you?"

"Another song!"

He knew he had to lower his expectations. Everyone has to live with repetitions. This is a way of learning and a way of enjoying the world.

"Oh, alright then," he said, mustering a grin.

"There were *three* clear jam jars, sitting on the skip!"

No, once he started singing, he always liked it. Perhaps he had a good voice.

Jas could easily push the bottles through this time. She laughed heartily as the first two disappeared and smashed.

When she came to the remaining one, they both sang, "One clear jam jar, sitting on the skip!"

At the last moment Jas said, "Lie-Lie wants in".

These childish names – but he had started it. Somehow from his Gee-Gee for a long-forgotten horse Jas had moved to the double-syllable menagerie.

She dropped the plastic animal, a lion, into the jar and, before Graham could stop her, thrust captive and container into the skip.

Father and daughter heard the glass smash.

Jas laughed but then stopped.

"My lion wants out now, Daddy," she said.

3

EARLY LEARNING CENTRE

GRAHAM TOOK ADVANTAGE of Jas's sobs by pushing the remaining bottle, forged from blue glass, into the white skip marked Clear. He was glad she didn't notice the anomaly. There were no skips for blue glass.

Jas struggled a little as he manoeuvred her into a better carrying position, then resigned herself to quiet tears on his shoulder.

They walked away from the recycling station and now and again she cried out, "My lion wants out, Daddy!"

He murmured, "I know, I know.", Finally he said, "He'll be alright in there, Jas. Honestly, lions can look after themselves."

She considered this seriously, but when he added, "And I'll get you another one. Don't worry," she started to wail again. "I want *that* lion!"

Graham breathed in and said nothing.

As he walked out of the car park with his living bundle, past the supermarket and towards the mall, Jas's mood began to soften. She became more interested in a substitute. She had remembered there were plastic animals in the shop at London Zoo.

"*Can't* we go to the Zoo today?"

"We'll try the Early Learning Centre, first."

Just before the automatic doors of the mall they both said, "Open Sesame!" with a laugh.

The doors obeyed the command.

It reminded Graham of one of the family rituals he and his brother Andrew had shared with their father when they were children. Whenever anyone coughed, their father would say "It's not the cough that carries you off, it's the coffin they carry you off-in!" The boys would groan a consolidated groan: it was a real groan and the simulation of a groan.

Inside the shopping centre (as they used to call malls when he was a child), Graham set his daughter down and she walked beside him.

Without prompting, she softly took hold of his hand.

Their fingers were a little sticky with the diluted jam from the jars.

At easy listening low volume the mall's public address system was playing Thunderclap Newman's 'The Revolution's Here'.

There was a general bustle of shopperly mooch. One woman in a lime green gilet smiled at Jas in recognition, turning to scrutinise Graham as if to say, "So you're Linda's husband, are you?"

They passed an electronic goods shop and Graham noticed that all the televisions, though tuned to a spectrum of channels, were showing the news. Framed in each channel's house-style, every screen was displaying the same black and white still, a small island.

When they crossed the threshold of the Early Learning Centre together a small box mounted near the door gave a click. It counted the two of them as one.

They went straight to the stands holding the plastic animals. There were dinosaurs, insects, amphibians and aquatic crustacea. Graham liked the tree-frogs best, brightly-coloured dandies of green and orange. Their turret-eyes looked out in different directions. Many of the creatures were not in scale with each other – a shrimp could have snacked on a brontosaurus. There were very few mammals and certainly no big cats.

"Would you happen to have any lions?" Graham asked the assistant, a woman in her forties.

"You're the second person to ask me that today! They're making another sequel to the Lion King, right?"

"Oh. I, I don't know. But we'd like one anyway. Have you got any in storage?"

"Sorry. But I'll put an order in, now I know there's a demand."

Graham glanced at Jas to see how she was taking the news. She didn't seem upset.

"No, that's OK. Thanks anyway."

As they walked out together – Jas placid, biddable for the moment – the machine at the door again clicked. Again, just the once.

The Who's "Won't get fooled again" was playing quietly on the mall's PA.

Graham was annoyed and then annoyed at being annoyed.

"You think too much," Linda had told him, "Which means you don't think enough about the important things."

Graham was annoyed about being annoyed at being annoyed.

The next shop they tried was a bookshop with a children's section.

In the middle of this there was an old-fashioned rocking-horse. Riding it was a girl of eight or nine, too big for the animal Graham thought, but he could see she was deliberately taking care to be gentle. She was shaking her shiny blonde hair and laughing with a peculiar laugh. It was a laugh which, though it was uncertain of itself – seeking confirmation that riding a rocking horse was truly as good and fun a thing to do as she thought it was – was all the same a laugh which had no intention of stopping.

Shoppers turned around and stared before slowly returning to their browsing. Graham expected the girl to say something, to shout out to whoever was with her.

No words issued. She appeared alone.

Jas moved off to the audio tapes shelves where she could recognise images from TV reproduced on the inlay cards.

Seeing her among the logos, he thought of the photograph of the island that he had seen on the sets in the mall. He was unsettled by this mental recurrence. Like the girl on the rocking-horse, there was something out of kilter about the image. His pre-cognitive senses registered disquiet without his intelligence being able to articulate just what the problem was.

Graham reached into his pocket, scooped his phone out and switched it on. Once it had warmed up it beeped and vibrated twice. It presented a little envelope sign on the screen, declaring "1 message received".

He opened the in-box and read the text.

"Give us a call. And."

Graham erased the message, changed the mode to vibrate only, put the keyboard protection on, and slipped the phone back into his pocket. He didn't know why he had switched his mobile on in the first place. He was embarrassed at the beeping. Even the children's section of a bookshop he regarded as sacred as a library. He'd call his brother later.

At least the office hadn't called and left a message. The island couldn't be his story.

He was surprised that most of the tapes were not covered in cellophane, packet-of-cigarettes style. Jas had disgorged each of the many cassettes from its box.

He began looking for the Lion King books.

Across the shop, a six-foot little Simba the Lion Prince, a sculpture in cardboard, was just what he had in mind. He left Jas to her tapes.

He was soon disappointed: the angular bucket at the base of the lion was half full of Harry Potter figurines, with no big cat in sight. Simba's dump-bin had been recycled. Even the Harry Potters appeared rather shop-worn, and the presence among them of a single Darth Vader suggested this display was used by the bookshop as the last holding place before bin really did mean bin.

A scan of the adult fiction shelves nearby found no Lion King volumes, never mind plastic lions. All the Harry Potter books were there, as well as some early Martin Amises, and a few books based on the Magic Roundabout.

Graham began to feel unlucky.

As he returned to Jas and helped her match the right tapes to the right inlay cards, he wondered if Linda would have fared better. He knew she would.

"Yes," he answered himself, imagining her voice, "Your tributes to me are always double-edged."

He put the last tape back on the shelf, not stopping to alphabetise.

The blonde girl on the rocking-horse was now moving the horse with an energy that threatened its bearings.

The shoppers paid no attention. Graham saw a small woman in her early twenties step away from the nearby Travel section. She went over to the rocking horse and lifted the girl off.

"She's not a show-jumping horse, Zara!" she said, kindly.

Graham saw she was the girl's mother. He saw that Zara could only have understood her own name and perhaps the word "horse" in her mother's simple sentence. Her head was just slightly too small for her body; her jogging pants were bulked up with the oversize nappy they concealed. She couldn't walk without her mother's help. She was obviously, obviously now, a child with severe brain damage.

Zara laughed with a strange low hum as the woman hugged her to take her off the horse, staggering a little.

"Simba's not a real lion, anyway." Jas said, and father and daughter walked out of the shop.

4

CLINGING

GRAHAM'S SWEAT HAD cooled. It seemed to be seeping back out of his sweatshirt onto his skin, making the drenched top stick here and there with a cold touch.

"That's clinging!" Graham and Andrew used to say to each other. The word was pronounced with an ambiguous last syllable, somewhere between -ing and simply -en, the Germanic 'clingen'.

It meant something that was so revolting it was funny. They'd shriek, close their eyes, tense their muscles in a deliberate spasm.

"That's clinging!"

Their mother would say gently – "Boys, don't be disgusting!" – and all save their father laughed. He'd look annoyed instead.

Graham knew now, after only these few years with Jas, this had been a pose. He was laughing by not laughing, not allowing himself to share. "Soppy-stern" Philip Larkin had called it: at the heart of their father's response was a gentleness so finely-adjusted the boys couldn't possibly have been sensitive to it.

The brothers had two other rhyme companions for 'clinging'.

'Minging' introduced the concept of odour to the sense of disgust, 'clinging' was more adhesion than smell. Something which was 'minging' was a very smelly thing indeed, with a thick, low smell. When you said it, you more barked it than anything else; it had a broad, mannish sense of humour to it. Only a word from another less fertile rhyme family, 'bowfing', suggested anything more comprehensively disgusting.

'Ginging', with a hard first g, was 'minging''s camp sibling. Smell was the thing with it, too, but it suggested a high gamey odour. While minging could be used as part of an insult, 'You're mingin', pal, and so's your trainers!', ginging was just too effete to be aggressive. Graham and Andrew had serious arguments, and they had jokey arguments: whatever the confrontation was it would end there and then if either of them resorted to 'ginging'. That word brought conciliatory eye-contact, tensionless absurdity. They'd laugh.

Recently, Linda had bought Jas a DVD of the German children's classic, *The Singing Ringing Tree*. Graham remembered the fun he and Andrew had had with the words in that title, watching it on the telly when they had been just too old for it.

Linda had upbraided him for using bad language in front of Jas before. Once he'd actually found himself shouting at Jas the choice sentence, "Sit on your arse for just one minute, can't you!" - but even he could refrain from using 'clinging', 'minging', and 'ginging' this time.

The old black and white serial he remembered had actually been shot in colour. It had lovingly-realised costumes: a man in an unconvincing but endearing bear suit; a stylised giant fish, as if a fifteenth century woodcut had used a goldfish to picture a dolphin.

It had basic, startling, effects: a princess was made 'ugly' by switching her with another, older, actress and colouring her hair green; thorn-bushes grew to the size of barricades in seconds; a balmy pool was transformed in a few blinks to an ice-bound waste. Finally, the dead stick of the sacred tree was triumphantly brought back to ringing life. The acting was so expressive the strange German language the actors used only made the sense of enchantment stronger.

Although Linda had bought the DVD herself, she seemed angry when he and Jas stayed in one afternoon to watch every episode on it.

"That's your idea of quality time with Jas, isn't? Watching TV!"

He could see Jas had found it as magical as he had. They looked at each other. Both said nothing.

"Are you going to win a million in money?" Jas said.

Graham used the drier parts of his sweatshirt to soak up the perspiration, untucking himself by accident, then tucking himself back in.

He rubbed his left shoulder to ease the tension there and thought involuntarily of Linda's shoulders: he still liked to move his lips across them when they were in bed, taking in the scent of her hair and the remains of her perfume, distilled by the day. Her skin was fine skin, she was strong.

Linda always took this to be his wordless invitation to make love. Graham wasn't sure himself if it was or not. He would hardly say no if Linda began tender reciprocation. Because she had long ago seen it as something more obvious than perhaps it was, it had become so. As it became clear to him, or so he thought, that she regarded that kind of active intimacy with a substantial degree of reluctance, they made love less and less. She saw it, he imagined, as a duty. He risked flattering himself she'd enjoy it once she'd conceded consent but knew she would judge making love a hopeless contender against a full night's untroubled sleep.

He became more and more determined to keep himself turned away from her. He'd wait like that, night after night, to see if, just once, she'd offer him a gentle invitation, an invitation the like of his roving soft kiss, her fingers or nose and lips on his skin, a caress or a nuzzle. He'd concentrate on *not* doing the same old thing, on not becoming an object of duty to her.

She did not approach him in that way. Instead, after weeks of abstinence, she turned around and said, resignedly, "I don't mind if you fancy it tonight."

He observed himself swallowing his pride, embittered but still excited by her.

That set the pattern.

Sometimes, when he simply could not wait for even this, he would turn over and his lips would touch her nape and shoulders in a copy of the old way. Hopefully she'd say something like "My services required tonight, are they?", softly but hurtfully, and they'd be together again, finally, once more.

Sometimes she'd say, "You never stop do you?", and depending on the tone of her voice this could mean yes and it could mean no.

"Are you going to win a million in money?" Jas said.

He was glad of the change of subject. Lions weren't everything, even in Jas's world.

"That's a good idea!"

He reached into his jeans and took out a pound coin, handed it to her.

"Let's go!"

At the Lotto table he filled in the form with a little green plastic pen. The pen was bound with Sellotape to a piece of hairy string, in turn anchored to one of the tensioned clips that held the red, white and blue structure together. Graham saw it as a burlesque of a chained book in a cathedral library. Certainly, the flimsy plastic pen was likely to be worth more than the religious text of the lottery slip.

Other people had special numbers for the lottery: on that principle, he should have, say, number six for D-Day (the 6th of June was the day his father used to say was the best day for a house move). Or thirteen for Jas's birthday. But he hated the thought of using numbers that had a human resonance – his own daughter for heaven's sake. The lottery was a dehumaniser, and people-as-numbers only colluded with its statistical hopelessness. It was hardly Agamemnon slaughtering his daughter for the chance that the gods might grant a sea-breeze, but he knew he was low when he stooped to fill in the lottery form: he'd be lower still if he started bringing Jas's own numerological being into the squalor of it.

A million pounds, a few million pounds.

He might simply hand it all to Linda and say, "It's the end, you know."

Blood money.

He wasn't sure she'd even accept it.

He wasn't sure if a win like that would mean the certain end of their marriage or the chance of its renewal.

"I'm leaving."

That little sentence was like a terrible satanic prayer, the mirror-side of "Jesus wept", an internal whisper which made the coals of Graham's synapses glow then burn.

He made the single downward stroke between the Lucky Dip brackets. Graham always chose the Lucky Dip because if the computer chose his numbers for him, that was one failure he couldn't be directly responsible for, wasn't it?

He gave the form to the Bangladeshi girl at the machine and tried to make eye contact with her. Jas handed her the pound coin and the assistant smiled down.

The girl gave her the freshly printed ticket, smiled at Jas again, and said, "Next, please."

"I'll have that, if you please," Graham said, not quite snatching it from Jas.

"The estimated jackpot for tonight is £5.6 Million," the ticket declared, in capitals.

He was glad to see that the six numbers the machine had chosen for him held no emotional significance. Even the relationship of these digits to each other seemed patternless. This was satisfyingly unaesthetic.

"Do you think we'll win, Dad?"

"No."

They both laughed. They always said this.

"Time for an Elephant Juice?" he asked her.

"Yes!"

5

AFRICAN ELEPHANT OR INDIAN ELEPHANT?

THE CAFÉ WAS busy.

Graham thought they might have to sit in the squalid smoking section.

As a psychological diversion he hoped would avert chain-smoking rebellion in Jas's teenage years, he encouraged his daughter to pity rather than resent smokers – "It's not their fault, Jas, they're just not very well". He was irritated at the selfishness of public smokers, propelling all those waste-products into everybody's air. He wanted Jas to be adolescent so he could conspiratorially up the anti, "Yeah, smokers, they wouldn't be too pleased if I pissed on their shoes, but they're happy to push a hundred or more toxic chemicals right into my lungs. And they call *non*-smokers kill-joys!"

His work meant he was more sensitive than most to airborne mortality. The image of the island on the televisions crossed his mind, and he wondered again if there was a connection with the Department. Perhaps he should be phoning in to see if Blue Shift were covering it. But they hadn't contacted him and he had to stop letting work get in the way of his life.

They joined the queue behind a man who was playing, with

one hand, with his car-keys, tapping them on the glass surface of the counter. With the other hand he was on the phone.

"The usual place. With this queue, by the time I've ordered coffee you'll probably be here. I've got the car."

Pause.

"Officially, overtime."

Pause

"No danger."

Pause.

"Bye. Love you."

The man rested his keys on the counter and folded the petite grey and turquoise phone with a snap, placing it in his pocket.

"African elephant or Indian elephant?" Graham asked Jas, speaking normally but feeling suddenly abnormal.

A surge of anger shot through him as if all the different tissues in his body knew the man in front of them, brain, blood, skin, muscle, organs and lymph.

And hated him.

For a moment he knew this man without knowing who the man was.

"Large ears today, Dad," she said, waving her hands at the side of her head.

The queue was moving slowly. Graham even in his bewilderment saw a couple vacate one table. Before he could ask Jas to go and sit there it was taken by a woman and her small son. With a note of exasperation yet do-good-ery, Jas consoled her father – "Never mind! I'll find another one." She moved quickly out into the midst of the tables and waited next to two elderly women who were about to leave.

The queue moved on and the man in front, who Graham

now saw had a simple silver ear clip at the top of his right ear, moved up a place without picking up his keys. He had taken his phone out again and was tapping a text into it. As he did this, Graham realised, without consciously recognising any detail of hair colouring, of complexion, of clothing – without recognising any distinguishing element to this random bag of human cells in front of him – Graham realised that this man, this everyday man in an everyday queue for everyday stimulants, was the driver who earlier that morning had nearly killed his daughter.

He. had. to. be. punished.

In less than a second Graham knew how this was to be done.

He leaned over the counter to conceal his actions from those behind him. In the shaking cage of his left hand he enclosed the man's keys. Noiselessly, he picked them up.

He slipped out of the queue, gathered Jas in his tensed arms, and walked as if steadily out of the suffocating café.

6

"HERE WE GO LOOBY LOO"

"CAN YOU SEE any yellow cars?"

"There's one. I want to go back to the café."

Graham was trying to run without appearing to run.

"That's right."

It was the wrong car.

"See any other yellow cars?"

"There's one."

"More of a van, that one."

"There's Noddy's car. I want some milk, Dad. Mummy doesn't mind queues."

Without looking, Graham walked on, sweating with the crime, sweating with the weight of Jas in his arms.

"Any other yellow cars?"

"Do you think Looby Loo will be in the boot?"

"Could be. Any other yellow cars, sweetheart?"

"*Here we go looby loo, here we go looby light.*"

Graham looked behind.

No Ear-Clip Man.

He couldn't have realised what had happened. If he hadn't realised straight away it was the man in the queue with the little girl, did that mean he wasn't likely to realise now?

Graham slowed down. He glanced at the Noddy Car and saw that it was the bright yellow open-top which, earlier, had been a weapon of attempted murder.

"Actually, Jas, yes: let's go for a ride in Noddy's car."

7

T.W.A.

THE KEY SLIPPED perfectly into the ignition and the engine started smoothly.

Graham felt he'd just discovered a magic lamp, and he knew to rub and wish. He exalted in full voice with a phrase containing several swearwords he had never used wholly audibly in front of Jas. He called the driver a coffee-drinking mobile-using child-murderer who was obsessed with himself and spent a lot of time in his own intimate company. Words to that effect.

He remembered himself and ducked behind the absolutely transparent windscreen.

He saw that Jas was safely strapped in beside him, apparently oblivious to the minor felony of car theft and the capital crime of bad language. He readjusted his driving position so he could reach the pedals properly. He settled into the black leather seat, admired the white instrumentation and drove off sedately towards the automatic barrier.

Up ahead, the automatic barrier was blocking his way.

Graham thought about the automatic barrier blocking his way.

Without accelerating, he drove through the low-maintenance shrubbery next to the automatic barrier.

Japonica perhaps. Linda would know. Snapping so many bushes had released a pleasing aroma.

They entered the dilapidated High Street beyond the mall. As he would in Linda's car he reached for a CD to put in the player and found it was, of all things, a recording by Ted Hawkins.

"Ted!" he said, glancing at Jas. She knew from long drives to rare breeds farms Graham meant the singer not a cuddly toy.

He was relieved at his good luck: the familiar singer on the car stereo would keep things normal. Jas shouldn't be alarmed.

Although Linda and Graham were from villages very close to each other, religious segregation meant they had only met in their late teens, when they were arts students at the University. Once, much later, left to his own awkward devices at a children's party, Graham had said to one of Linda's friends, "Ted Hawkins introduced us."

"A world music DJ mentioned that Hawkins was playing a small club in Glasgow, and we both turned up for the gig. Ironic that we'd practically been neighbours for years. And at the same university – but it was radio and a rough and ready singer-songwriter from the States that brought us together."

Linda's friend seemed interested in a kind way.

The late Ted Hawkins.

The programme had been a staple of background music for them as they studied into the night. The DJ had championed the ex-con beach bum, encouraging him to make an album. Independently of each other Linda and Graham had felt part of that campaign, hearing the new recordings the presenter had commissioned.

Playing now as Graham brought the complicated sliders on the stereo to a level horizontal line Ted Hawkins' most famous song, "Watch your Step". This was an angry even misogynistic outcry but many of Hawkins's songs had the pathos of someone appearing to hope too much. One was a real-time monologue in which the singer told his sick girlfriend that he was going down to the off-licence to get just the medicine she needed. It didn't matter how much it cost, though, boy, you could tell Hawkins knew poverty – and she'd be as right as rain, she needn't worry. Everyone but Hawkins could be confident that this was a hopeless case. Perhaps the scrupulousness with which the singer outlined what he was going to do suggested that he, too, was not really fooled. In the face of the inevitable he had already fallen into the comforting arms of meticulous procedure. It was no good him asking, "What do you want from the liquor store?" – that woman was already as good as a corpse.

Graham drummed in time on the little sports steering wheel, as he always did in their boxy car, and Jas groaned, "Dad!", as she always did.

Linda and Graham had both arrived early at the club, a modest-sized dance floor near Queen Street Station. Linda recognised Graham as someone who simply looked familiar, a feeling which was the consequence perhaps of the many times their lives must have overlapped unknowingly at home and now on campus. It was as if the senses had a form of recognition which, though weak, is stronger than the powers of conventional memory. Graham thought it was this same super-perceptive sense that had made him identify the driver of this Noddy car.

In a room where students were outnumbered by much

older people, all men, Linda had felt this vague superficial sympathy with Graham and had gone over to him.

"'T.W.A.''s my favourite," she said, without offering a "Hello!".

"Mine too!" Graham replied, taking up the implied question.

"T.W.A." was an extremely short song, a paean to the eponymous airline. Perhaps Hawkins had intended it as a jingle, in the hope it would feature in a commercial. The royalties alone would release him, he may well have prayed, from his near-vagrant life.

The demise of the air company, and Hawkins' own death now, made the song one of those innocent records tainted with the melancholy of a knowledge beyond itself. It was like the plaintive seagulls dubbed onto Otis Redding's "Sitting on the Dock of the Bay", just days before his fatal aircraft accident, seagulls he never got to hear. Graham, not one to pause at the threshold of a gloom-party, also drew Linda's attention to John Lennon's unassuming single "Just Like Starting Over", released weeks before his murder.

Linda and Graham would find themselves singing "T.W.A." for many years after first hearing it.

Before Jas's birth, Linda would never sing with anyone else in the room. It was an intimate privilege for Graham to hear her through the distortion of a shower and the bathroom door, extolling unselfconsciously the benefits of transcontinental flight. That softly-spoken educated accent he adored! He'd fight the impulse to join in, knowing that if she heard him, she'd stop immediately.

There was no support band and Hawkins failed to appear on stage at the billed time. A spokesman announced that air traffic control problems in London had delayed the singer's arrival at Glasgow Airport.

"We're expecting Ted on stage in forty-five minutes."

"Typical English!" Linda joked to Graham, "They're always stopping our fun!"

"It's OK to have their nuclear weapons twenty miles west of Glasgow, but they grudge us Ted!" Graham replied.

He was surprised at how much edge there was to his voice when he talked about the military base, almost as surprised as he was by his referring to the singer by his first name. He thought Linda might immediately take him for a nationalist on the hard left of the party (at that time, Graham had no well-formed political opinions at all). Worse – for a reader of those newspapers who, with a familiarity as offensive as their lack of discrimination, deploy Christian names for rock stars and murdered children alike.

The delay meant Linda had been worried about getting back home. She knew her mother would wait up for her, and she herself would now be forced to kill time in the dead hour between the end of the day timetable and the start of the night buses.

Graham, who had the loan of his mother's car that night, quickly volunteered to make sure Linda got home safely. He was amused at the coincidence of their living in neighbouring villages. At a phone near the cloakroom Linda was able to persuade her mother to seriously consider going to bed, if no more could be expected than the contemplation at least.

Ted Hawkins arrived an hour later, simply walking across the dance floor up on to the stage and starting with the minimum of fuss. Graham noticed that his guitar had a capo, a foreshortening of the strings he'd later associate with the singer's intense life, and with Hawkins' death less than a decade later.

A tall, well-built black man with a grey-flecked beard, Hawkins immediately won over his audience with an apology and the remark, "They lied about the Scottish weather! There ain't no rain in Glasgow tonight!"

Then he hollered "Watch your step!" And the gig of Linda and Graham's lifetime started.

The M25 was slow-moving as Graham and Jas drove on to the city-bound lane.

The M8 was quiet as Graham and Linda drove back towards home. They hardly talked about the concert. Instead, they chattered away about their studies and their strangely parallel school days, separated by a few arable fields, a bypass, and what they agreed was a kind of apartheid.

"You lot stoned our school bus!" Graham told her.

"You lot put Paddies Go Home across our school wall!"

When they neared Kilpeter, Linda said, "No, drive that way," meaning up towards the Clyde. On a road overlooking the beginning of the Firth, she asked Graham to pull over and they sat for a moment staring out at the ancient citadel of Dumbarton on the other side of the estuary. It was illuminated in points of yellow.

"That was the capital of all Strathclyde once." Graham said, as if naturally.

He was aware of Linda's perfume, softened by an evening's diffusion. When he turned round to look at her, he was taken aback at the tenderness of light in her blue eyes, a soft grey now in the countryside night.

"Governing all the south-west of Scotland, and with a sister state in Cumbria," he went on. Linda just about smiled.

There was a pause.

"Can you guess what language the inhabitants spoke here in 600 AD, Miss Political Science?"

She looked at him in recognition of the nonsense of it, this speaking for speaking's sake.

"Irish?" she said, with a hint of chauvinism.

"Welsh, Linda McGourty. An early kind of Welsh. Brythonic."

"Should Plaid Cymru be campaigning tonight?"

She leant over and kissed him on the lips, gently running her tongue along the moist bottom edge of his top lip. He reached out and held her in his arms and they kissed for a few minutes.

He moved his lips gently across her tired face, his nose almost snuffling along the line of her hair ("Chestnut hair," he thought, and thought of The Byrds' 'Chestnut Mare'). He dwelt at the soft skin behind her ear, kissing the top edge of her ear and nosing about with such enthusiasm she said, "My ear is not the only food in the trough, you know!"

She undid the first few buttons on her blouse and reached behind herself to undo the clip of her bra. She directed Graham's head to her liberated left breast and slid her right hand under the top edge of his jeans.

Graham moved her loosened bra down further with his nose.

When he was fifteen he'd once said to a reluctant girlfriend, "Your bra's a parachute!"

"Why's that?" she'd said.

"I thought it was never going to open!"

Graham felt now that he and Linda were both now in that half-comic, half-exalted rush of free-fall.

Graham moved his hand beneath the waistband of her skirt and beneath the simple cotton of her knickers, touching the softly pressed hair there.

Linda seemed to be in a hurry.

She stopped to take her skirt and knickers off, and Graham undid the buckle of his jeans and stripped from the waist down. They moved onto the vinyl bench seat in the back of the car, leaving their clothes in the front. They laughed at the coolness of the plastic as it touched their bottoms.

Only a few minutes later, Linda said "Mum!" and they dived into the front.

For a second, he actually thought her mother was outside the car.

"I mean look at the time," Linda added. Graham looked at the clock embedded in the dashboard. It didn't seem that late.

"I'd better get home," Linda continued.

They didn't bother with their underwear, except for Linda's bra, and they slipped the rest of their clothes on quickly.

Linda scrunched her knickers up, wiped herself with them, and put them in her handbag.

When he dropped her off in front of her house in Kilpeter Linda pointed to a curtained window with a light behind it.

"That's me," she said. "Looks like Mum is still up."

"That a problem?"

"Not really. She thinks I'm a good wee girl, more or less! I'll tell her there was an extra delay because we went via the Clyde Tunnel."

Graham returned her smile with half a laugh. He was excited that a woman could talk like that.

"And that you're at the top of your year. She thinks good results are a hallmark of character."

"Thanks for a lovely evening," Graham said.

Linda looked at him and slowly sung the first line of "T.W.A."

She broke off, laughed, kissed him on the cheek, and quietly closed the car door.

Graham took the car out of neutral, turned it around, and headed for home.

Graham drove further and further away from home, towards the junction for the city. He dropped down to third as the traffic ahead showed its crimson brake lights. He wondered if he was technically kidnapping Jas as well as stealing the car. A convoy of armoured vehicles with a police escort encouraged the traffic to move out of their way.

"Naughty boys!" Graham and Jas said together, the family refrain whenever a police car's panicky siren sounded. The convoy left the motorway at the Heathrow slip road.

The traffic began to increase its speed a little and Graham was able to move up to fourth gear.

8

KEY-HOLE SURGERY

GRAHAM FELT COLD with the wind buffeting around him. Worse, the motorway seemed more edgy than usual. Even with the music up high, in the open-top the noise of the cars and especially the lorries menaced and unnerved him.

He was surprised that the danger of a collision concerned him more than being caught by the authorities (or the car's owner himself). Being in the car, even in a glorified chassis like this little cabriolet, seemed to insulate him against the merely metaphysical worry of judgement. The material vulnerability of the car itself, the fragility of its current occupants, were more pressing anxieties: the tailgates of lorries could easily decapitate him if he misjudged the breaking distance.

Perhaps Jas would escape.

Looking across and smiling to disguise his thoughts, he judged, yes, Jas was small enough to survive that kind of accident. On the other hand, perhaps she was not large enough to wear the adult seatbelt which now lay across her like a loose sash. She had never been allowed to sit in the front before: she still rode in a child seat in the rear in fact. For the moment she was enjoying the view of the backs of vehicles and the breeze touching the top of her hair.

"Are we going to the Zoo, Dad?" she asked, nearly shouting to make herself heard. Graham felt ghoulish to have been thinking of her death, even if he was thinking about its avoidance.

"Too right we are!" Graham tried to sound as if that was the plan all along.

"Plenty of lions, there. Real ones!"

"And plastic ones?"

"And plastic ones."

Jas announcing her own priorities like that, Graham thought of the girl on the rocking horse in the bookshop. She would be unable to say anything as specific as "Are we going to the Zoo, Dad?" She would be unable to say anything at all.

No, you couldn't give up on folk like that. Perhaps her mother had developed a calibration of understanding fine-tuned to non-verbal cues, eyes looking briefly at a desired object, a facial expression that meant not just boredom but a precise depth of boredom, a laugh whose timbre showed it had understood a simple joke.

Graham remembered the sense he had of her appealing to anyone around her, asking for their tacit consent to enjoy herself. Though he had seen the girl for only a few seconds, he felt sure she was able to communicate highly nuanced social concepts.

If parents really understood the risks of having children, the chances of having children more severely handicapped than that girl, of course most would still have them. Conception was not a rational act. He and Linda had been determined to be parents without understanding more than the compulsion. When it began to dawn on them that they might not in fact be able to have children, rationality had, though, brought their emotional state down from anguish to philosophical resignation, from bitterness to a kind of acceptance. They would try the simplest of medical remedies, minor surgery even, but weren't prepared to pursue the gradually cranked-up distress of IVF.

After he had been tested, as he had called it, even when talking to himself, and been found reassuringly average, it was Linda's turn for scrutiny.

A "small exploratory operation" the doctor told her.

Before going to the hospital, post-operation, Graham had written out some lines of a poem he'd found in an anthology, partly as a lucky charm, partly in solidarity. As he was setting it out on a card (he'd found a flowery one in Linda's stationery drawer) some doggerelish rhymes came into his head and he added them as a post-script, his own poem. He left the card with some flowers while she slept, post-op.

When he was permitted to see her again, he told her, "It's so much easier to say it in poetry, because poetry has silences you can fill, if you want to."

Linda was pale; her fingers, when Graham reached out to touch, hold them, were frail and dry. "I'm not feeling too poetic. But thanks for the card, and the words, your words, and the flowers." Linda smiled, looking at the vase and its mass of yellow periscopes. "I wondered lonely as a daffodil."

"Have they told you anything yet?"

"They didn't find anything. I don't know whether to laugh or cry."

But Graham could hear in her voice the edge of a sob. He had never heard her cry.

They looked at each other reassuringly as they talked,

Linda substantial to Graham in her fragility. It was a state of being he had not encountered before. It was as if he was missing her, just as he missed her when they couldn't be together – work trips or separate visits to family – but without needing distance now to know how much he loved her. They were hand-in-hand in their lives together, in each other's arms, as if he was seeing for the first time that the sleepwalking marriage of living together was as near to sacred as his unbelieving sensibility could be expected to appreciate.

Linda-and-Graham was desire and friendship and even brother-and-sister, recurrent moments of that order of idealism.

The strength of her vulnerability – the tiny intricate bonds of their life together, multitudinous, delicate each in themselves, the single chords that together kept a structure like the Erskine Bridge suspended gracefully in air!

"Anyway, it might not matter."

"How do you mean?"

"They don't know why, but a significant percentage of patients have a child soon after the operation –"

Graham interrupted her with a quizzical look

"—apparently, yes. Even when it's inconclusive like mine."

They were silent for a few moments.

"Well, we've both at least passed the test," he said. "I think it's going to be OK—"

"You've an average squirt," Linda whispered, looking round at the other patients, busy with their families, "and I've an average belly – on the inside!"

Graham adored Linda's slight, slight paunch.

"And if it's not OK, we're not going to get all het up. We're not going to drive ourselves to desparation."

"And there's nothing wrong with your belly, inside or out! If Josephine had had a belly like yours, Napoleon would never have bothered with all that conquering palaver, the Germans wouldn't have harboured subsequent simmering resentments against the French, and, in short, the First and Second World War would both have been averted. Fact. Napoleon would simply have stayed indoors, a-carressing and a-canoodling – or, as the French say, '*canoodlhuissant.*'"

"Your language skills are as bad as your history, Gray. But thank God they're not as bad as your taste in women."

In the afternoon, once the gynaecologist had repeated what a junior member of staff had told her before Graham had arrived, Linda was free to go.

Graham wheeled her to their Ford, carefully shimmied her into the front passenger seat, clicked her into the seat belt, and drove her home.

Graham drove further and further away from home.

More army traffic appeared on the opposite lane, light armoured vehicles again. There were several unmarked cars that Graham knew to be for higher ranking military officials.

Trapped between two high-sided coaches, he missed the first junction for the city.

9

AN AGENDA

JAS WAS PLAYING nicely with the tiger.

The glove compartment made a perfect cave once the London A-Z and stock of CDs had been removed. She knew the alphabet and was able to read common words. Inside the book she had been surprised to see just lines and incomprehensible tiny writing going this way and that.

Graham looked briefly at the CDs and saw many he had in his own collection.

In the games Jas played with her toys she herself was a character: sometimes she took on the role of a horse, sometimes a unicorn; always with the gift of speech. Most often, as with today, she was a princess about to be married.

"When I grow up, I'm going to marry you Dad!" she said, "And Tiger will be in the audience!"

"I thought Tiger was called Tie-Tie?" Graham replied, ignoring the complications of marriage to his own daughter.

"Oh, that was just his pretend name. That's just baby talk."

Graham realised he had missed the first opportunity to get off this motorway for the road that led into town. He was conscious of his own dislocation from the theft of the car, as if the beauty of the car and the music and the existence of his daughter justified it all. Revenge was a distant feeling now, a freak flood of merely historic interest.

He was as relaxed as the resolution of a family advertisement. He knew the next city-bound junction was coming up soon enough, and was content to listen to country blues, to hear Jas with her up-on-tip-toes accent for royalty.

She was adopting true fairy-tale tactics and putting a few inter-species difficulties in the path of her wedding story: tiger, princess, princess, tiger – how could they kiss if all Tiger wanted was to eat human flesh.

When Graham had first known Linda, they were both very conscious of keeping marriage and its desperate hopes at a distance from them. He wasn't sure if they were afraid of their own sentimentality or afraid of committing to something whose seriousness they would not be able to fathom without plunging into it.

'Marriage isn't on the agenda at present': Linda's phrase in their university days. Graham felt led by her. When he talked to his mother he began to use the phrase, too.

He didn't know why he had been keener to tie the knot than Linda appeared to be. When he thought he was being honest with himself, he wasn't sure he loved her wholeheartedly. He loved her, he was sure he loved her, but he could not master that concept of unconditional love required, he thought, by the idea of marriage, whether conceived sacredly, romantically, or within a humanistic framework of social and civil declaration. He guessed Linda shared these misgivings.

Did this mean their standards were too high, or too low?

He thought he felt passionate when she was wearing a new outfit. He was certainly passionate when he was helping her to take one off.

"I'm at the mercy of a lust dependency," he told himself, writing the phrase down on a receipt.

He was thinking of lyrics that might one day appear on an indie record. He put a line break after "mercy" for suspense and a shuffling rhyme, but he couldn't think of a tune. He wasn't sure whether he was writing in a local Scottish tradition – he was conscious of how self-aggrandising it was calling himself a 'songwriter' on the basis of a single couplet – or whether he had latched onto an English or, worse, American, idiom.

He wondered whether there was a difference between the English and Scottish traditions of literate bands. He had made a note in his Augustans and Romantics folder:

> *Smiths: guitar noises, witty (Aug.?), English accent important, lonely*
>
> *Blue Nile: keyboard noises, earnest (Rom.?), Scottish accent important, lonely*
>
> *Concept of body-loneliness.*
>
> *"Yearn": out-dated word. Reason?*

The lyric text on the receipt was later erased during a service wash at his local laundry, but he would always remember it: "One of my finest couplets, that."

Years later, just before Jasmine, he lost a lottery ticket in much the same way, though they had their own washing machine by then. He had no recollection of the actual numbers – as always, they were chosen randomly by Lucky Dip – but it was a joke between Linda and Graham that he had probably lost the jackpot.

"How dare you steal my treasure!" Jas shouted at the tiger. Graham thought how fickle she was with her friends. He raised a comic eyebrow that Jas did not see.

"Roar!" the tiger said, as if it knew the actual word.

Jas moved her hand towards what Graham could now see was a clear-green cigarette lighter behind the tiger.

"Rarrrhh!" the tiger said, with more volume and less elocution.

"I am a princess! Give it to me."

The tiger stood his ground.

"Give it to me!"

The tiger looked up a little.

"Give it to me!"

The tiger miaowed and moved away.

"Good boy!" Jas picked up the lighter. "You can marry me," she said, sweetly.

The tiger purred and would have said thank you, Princess Jasmine, but tigers weren't yet able to talk in the story.

At university every so often Graham would ask Linda to marry him. The occasion was usually connected with the consumption of beer from bottles with porcelain clamps for bottle-tops. Strong.

"The whole thing – church, marquee, Milan."

She'd say, "We're so young Graham."

A week after his father had been killed in a car accident, Graham had proposed without benefit of drink. There was an edge to his voice, and he didn't mention Leonardo's Last Supper.

Linda varied the response – "Sweet boy," – but he knew that that meant No, too.

He still asked her, "Does that mean No?"

"That means No," she said.

During Graham's final year, his brother Andrew married a local girl, Georgie. They moved to Newcastle after a winter wedding and Graham saw much less of him. Andrew would visit their mother in her village but not have time to drop in on Graham in Glasgow.

Andrew was a fine phoner, though. There were so many problems to do with the safety: productivity ratio in Andrew's line of work and Andrew needed a listener. Pharmaceuticals were less scientific and more businesslike than Graham had imagined.

He felt useful. It was like a tape recording of a conversation from the old days, an audio tape of the younger brother's Uh-huhs, Rights, and Reallys as he handed Andrew tools through the carcass of any one of his scrap-rescued boy-racers.

But he still felt isolated. He visited Andrew and Georgie in Newcastle a few times. In places the city was red sandstone like Glasgow, and the folk were like the Weegies: they knew how to shop, they knew how to drink, and they knew how to talk. Graham wrote in his James Joyce folder that he would like shopping and drinking more if they led to people not away from them.

Ditto for too much study, and, he already knew, ditto for lying night after night in the strong arms of Linda McGourty.

He had quickly grown apart from his old school friends. Most had evaded university courtesy of work shy giggles and soft drugs. Those who could complete the forms successfully

– an exam was a form – had gone to universities far out of the area, to England or even to Edinburgh.

Graham's obsession with Linda meant he hardly made any new friends. His life was lectures, study, Linda, lectures, study, Linda, lectures, study . . . and Linda. The only progression he could envisage was marriage.

He saw matrimony abstractly, as much in relation to literary tropes as to life. Dr. Marcus Appleton, Senior Lecturer, had said, "You can't understand English literature or British life today without knowing your Dante," and Graham thought that, yes, marriage was likely the yawn of the *Paradiso*. But surely it was also the only brave place left after *Hell* and *Purgatory*?

Though Graham was as sceptical of the Dante cult as he was of his lecturer's abilities, Dr. Marcus Appleton, Senior Lecturer, might just right. This was a teacher whose classes were more digression than explanation. Appleton was especially keen on correcting the consensus of contemporary speech. He said when you talked about the Celtic football team you had to pronounce it with a hard C. This was because the Greeks had fashioned the word for the Kelts, and the Greeks did not have the soft c in their alphabet.

For the same reason you had to say "Agenda" as if it had the hard g in "A Gander".

Dr. Marcus Appleton, Senior Lecturer, didn't realise that his accent made Aggenda and A Ggander aurally coterminous.

Graham said to Linda, "Oxford Appleton makes 'a list of business to be transacted at a meeting' indistinguishable from 'a male goose'."

Linda said, "Context is everything."

Graham and Linda shared a small high-ceilinged flat a few blocks west of the motorway. The skirting boards and dados ended abruptly where the original tenement had been partitioned. Graham regarded this as an aesthetic sacrifice that honorary working-class people like students had to make in solidarity with the overcrowded and the homeless.

To begin with, whoever came home first cooked. By luck, cooking for each other had a happy, even, distribution between them. During one term, when Linda had many free slots last thing, this changed, and she became the main chef.

Her favourite dish was spaghetti Bolognese. It was the only meal her mother had showed her how to prepare, the lesson occurring one Saturday in the summer before Linda left for digs. Linda told Graham that she had also given her *The Reader's Digest Manual of DIY* and a generous voucher for British Home Stores.

Linda repeated spaghetti Bolognese night after night.

After a week, Graham made some jokey comments about the monocuisine – "We'll both be descended from Italians by the end of our degree, like everyone else in Glasgow!" – but the next day it was Linda's "speciality" again.

Finally, one afternoon Graham skipped his last class. Since it was by the good Doctor Appleton, he regarded this as a low-risk strategy.

He bought some vegetables from a couple of the Pakistani shops along the Great Western Road, and a few small jars of exotic dried herbs from a mini-supermarket.

He set to work, scrubbing the traffic particulates off the raw ingredients with some washing up liquid and setting a pan for a minceless fry. Gradually a sauce accumulated: he had an aromatic dish ready just in time for Linda's return. It was bubbling beautifully – not, he hoped, with the remains of the detergent – and quick-boil rice cut the time for any nervous anticipation.

On their plates certain wood-like vegetables had to be isolated as clearly demanding further culinary expertise, the kind Graham did not yet possess, but they devoured the rest of the new food.

Linda would later tell the story against herself: "At last the cycle of violence was broken."

A couple of years later, a few weeks before graduation, Linda accepted a copy-writing job at a London advertising agency, GoldStandard.

"Are you coming?" she said to Graham, mock-brusquely.

He paused.

"There's nothing else on the Aggenda," he said.

They smiled, their eyes met, and she kissed him on the cheek.

They married at Camden Town Hall a few months after arriving in London.

"Is this the way to the Zoo?" Jas said.

"Yes." Graham replied, emphatically.

10

AND

AS HE GUIDED the car onto the slip road, his phone vibrated twice in his pocket. He decelerated towards the linking roundabout, tried to reach into his pocket as he let traffic pass. He didn't quite manage to retrieve the phone before the road cleared so he gave up on it. He steered round and up onto the motorway for the city. You had to be responsible with a young passenger in your car.

Once he was settled in the middle lane, traffic moving easily and quickly, he fished the phone out and read the message.

"It's The Island. Phone me. And."

Graham tapped down the phone's directory to Andrew's name, abbreviated. He knew his own name would be shortened in Andrew's electronic phone book, too.

They had been And and Gray since they were toddlers. And and Gray, plus and minus when he was feeling low. Jas was Jazz (you didn't have to spell it out), and Linda was always Linda.

He pressed the little phone icon, 'Call', but a large battery symbol appeared on the screen, flashed dully, greyly he thought, and the screen went blank.

He thought of the involuted psychiatric patients he'd read

about in last Saturday's papers. To do what they thought was saving themselves they simply, silently, turned themselves to the wall. It was their version of 'Leave me alone', not having to acknowledge anyone, including themselves, by actually saying it.

The phone always switched itself off to conserve the integrity of its memory. The memory was inaccessible to the outside world and, since the phone only properly existed when its master was using it, inaccessible to the phone itself. It was perfect isolation, as useless as purity.

"Was that Mummy, Dad? Does she know about our new car?"

"It was your Uncle And. But my batteries have gone dead."

"Oh, never mind," Jas said sympathetically, executing an accomplished unconscious impression of Linda, trying to avert tears and a tantrum. "It doesn't matter, really."

"I need to get off the motorway and find a phone box."

"There's a phone box at the Zoo." Jas said, authoritatively. "I think," she added.

"It might be urgent."

"Oh you'll never find one." Then, a flash of inspiration, "Oh – I mean, there's one."

Jas waved her tiger at an emergency phone point. It was by the steel barrier separating the burgundy hard shoulder from the greenish off-colour verge. When they were little, Andrew and Graham had pretended these phones were American-style mailboxes for long-distance lorry drivers.

Graham was about to say, "They're only for emergencies," but thought of a more precise definition: "They're only if you have a car accident."

"Could we have a gentle car accident?"

Graham thought of his father.

"It doesn't really work that way."

At the next junction, Graham came off the motorway and quickly found himself among down-at-heel light industrial units.

There was a record company with one wall painted in Rastafarian yellows, reds and greens, a firm which might have been a wholesale halal butcher, and several units whose names couldn't be securely linked to any particular trade. Some had 'Vacancies' signs, including one with a very specific need for a Sheet Metal Worker. Each had two or three parking spaces in front. Some had the thickly painted designation on the theme Reserved for Managing Director.

There were few cars. Saturday.

Some medium-sized vans were parked here and there, and in an old Japanese car a teenage driver was practising a three-point turn with a slightly older teenage girl at her side, sisters perhaps. As he passed them gingerly, Graham could see they were enjoying themselves, and they made brief eye contact. All smiled at layers of recognition: they had seen that he realised they had understood his nervousness. Graham was conscientious about his soft-top, even if it was, as he reflected with continued detachment, somewhat stolen.

"Can I have a car, one-day, Dad?" Jas said.

"You certainly can. But we'll be flying in mini space-ships by the time you're grown-up."

"I'd still like a car. For my holidays."

"What sort would you like?"

"A pink Jeep to go on safari."

Graham wasn't sure if he was on a through-road.

Perhaps he had missed a cue on the motorway indicating this turn-off was for a Trading Estate only. The word "lorry" occurred to him – the symbol would have been a lorry – and he thought for no reason in particular how much he liked that word. He almost said it out loud, like a screen village-idiot, 'Loh-ree.'

He drove further along the gently curving road which ended abruptly at the edge of a canal. There was no phone booth in sight. After he'd executed in his opinion an ostentatiously perfect three-point turn – if the learner girls could still see him! – he stopped the car. He was conscious of feeling a little cold now and worrying if Jas felt even colder. It wouldn't do any harm to put the roof up, especially as it might just disguise the car a little. He inwardly laughed at his own optimistic stupidity, but with a "There you are, I am stupid" sense of good humour.

He struggled with the black folded up roof at the back of the car. He used hands, arms, legs and feet for a few minutes before it occurred to him the process might be automated, the simple matter of a button on the control fascia. Hot now with his exertions (and once the car had stopped he realised how humid the weather was), he was nevertheless determined to succeed with this roof. Nothing on the panel served this purpose: he even switched the hazard lights on, knowing what that little triangle meant but imagining a whole different set of signs for little yellow cars.

Finally, he looked down below the driver's seat, hoping to find the sort of button that normally opens a bonnet but in this case would apply itself to the canopy.

There it was, with a little sign for a car with a lid. Within seconds the roof had magisterially raised itself, requiring only a few self-evident adjustments by hand to secure it. He sat back down in the driver's seat as if the day's mission had been completed.

"The Zoo definitely has a phone," Jas reminded him.

11

THE ISLAND

"NO PHONES, NO cars, no television, nothing but the sea and the sand."

Graham's father appeared to think these negatives amounted to a paradise. He was filling one of two huge white plastic containers with water from the bath's cold water tap.

"But it's your mother's holiday as much as yours, boys," he went on.

Graham and Andrew crowded around him.

They were like students of social history observing a retired but still skilled artisan. For the benefit of academic curiosity, the master craftsman was demonstrating an intricate process superseded long ago by mechanisation. The sound of the container changed as it filled.

"So you're on your best behaviour and there *will* be one or two more chores than usual."

"Aw, Dad!" both brothers groaned.

"Aw Dad nothing. You boys are the laziest shower of lazy layabouts I've ever known, and I've known quite a few!"

As he said this, their father seemed to draw on his whole career, from schoolboy raspberry-picking among field gangs, through white-coated colleagues in the polymer labs, and most of all to years of middle management.

The container was full. He reached out and snatched its cap from Andrew, who had been frenetically trying to make it spin on its side on the base of the bath.

"Maybe it's time you two learned to do more about the house and let your mother have some time to herself for a change." He pointed pointedly at Andrew with the cap.

"Aw, Dad!" Andrew said again, more softly than before, admitting in just those two words general defeat and even his own particular responsibility – without, though, offering anything in reparation that could be taken as specific.

"Can I have my own fishing rod for the holiday, Dad?" Graham piped up, as if he was now in a bargaining position. "A blue one with a clicky reel?"

"Can I, can I, can I!" his father replied, laughing and, to the boys, clearly repeating a phrase he'd laughed about alone with their mother. She was often the absent audience he appeared to play to when he was with them.

He gently placed the cap on to the container's top, feeling to avoid cross-threading it as if it were a carefully weighted camera lens, then he screwed it firmly into place.

"Can I go exploring, Dad?" Andrew asked.

Their father was disconnecting an empty water container in the motor-caravan's galley to replace it with the reserve. As he grinned to take the weight of the replacement cannister, manoeuvring it to join it up to the pipe, he glanced at Mum who just smiled.

She was relaxed, finally. It was the penultimate day of the fortnight.

She was waiting for some fresh water to pour into the flask

in her painting bag, watercolours today after finishing an oil yesterday.

Dad had already taken many shots of the same changing seascape, this filter on, this filter off.

Mum wanted to paint the same scene in watercolours, another experiment in variation.

"Perhaps without so much sand on the surface this time," she'd said.

"But the sand's magic," Gray told her. He could see that in fact she already felt that way, too.

She had been painting her latest oil just as a wind started to whip up. As the rest of the family retreated to the van, a look back showed the sandstorm had already blurred her to a determined smudge. When she finished the granulated painting she said: "It's like Manet or Eardley or something!"

It was the first time Graham had heard her being proud of something she had made, apart from the boys themselves. He knew she didn't mean literally like Manet or Eardley.

"What do you have in mind?" Dad asked, in a voice Andrew and Graham knew expressed consent. The jaunt was on, they were now merely talking terms.

"Going beyond the platform, along the shore. Or maybe getting straight up onto the moor first?"

"It's just after low-tide now, so get to the platform first. Leave the dry land until later so you don't get cut off by the tide. I want to try a crab or two for the last fishing so I'll be more or less just behind you in the rock pools. Near enough for a yell, anyway."

"Can I come, too?" Graham asked, as if to Mum, but knowing all three were involved. They could each say no for different reasons.

"I suppose so." Mum and Andrew said together.

His mother was hesitant, as if finely gauging Graham's capabilities, his physical strength, his common sense. His brother was reluctant, sensing all the same it was still strategic to offer something to secure the expedition.

"It'd be safer that way." Dad said.

"Yes!"

"And no swimming Andrew Urquhart, OK?"

The boys ran down past the large upturned boat, grassed over, a parliament in the rain for sheep. When they turned along the shore path, concealed from the caravanette by a drystone dyke, And stopped and pulled a rock out of the wall.

He reached into the hole and brought out a can of Sweet-Heart Stout.

"How did you get that all the way up here?"

"I put it in among my socks in my kitbag. Audrey's my favourite."

Audrey had dark brown hair and Gray thought she must be a swimming enthusiast with clothes like that.

"Are you sure you should be drinking on the way to the platform?" said the daddish Gray. "Those rocks are still slippy at low tide. Look what they were like the other day!"

"Don't be such a jessie."

"I'm not a jessie!"

"Aye ye are."

"No Ah'm no."

"Are."

"Areny."

"Are."

"Areny."

They walked along the grassy path. The day was warm but

they had the benefit of the sea breeze now, the beginning of the rock-pools beneath them.

"Are," And said quietly.

Gray tutted and momentarily raised his eyes in disgust.

And opened the can and lost some of the beer, lava.

He wiped Audrey carefully on the side of his cut-off jeans.

"Anyway, stout's good for you," he advised his younger brother. "Mum had stout when she had us at the infirmary."

"Can I have some, then?"

And took a gulp then handed Gray the can.

"Just a sip. Some things can be too good for you."

Gray had a careful taste and was going back for more when it was snatched off him.

"Let's save the rest for later."

The path rose and veered so that the immediate shore was lost to view. They were walking away from the beach of the painting, of their sprints and shell-hunts. They followed the path for several minutes before it found the sea-edge again and then they clambered down to a flat area of rock where they had been fishing over the holiday with their father.

They walked towards the edge of the rock and could see soft bright sea-colours they had not seen before, browns and greens, blues and yellows, sand and weed and rock out there, closer to the surface now. It was a clear day and they could see out across to mountains, gentle and austere at the same time. At the very edge of the platform both looked down, staring methodically into the lapping water ten feet beneath them.

"I can't see it, Gray."

"Maybe it'll be washed up on the beach?"

"It'd be ruined anyway. All rusted."

Gray said nothing, tightened his lips.

"Come on, let's have another sip."

Conscientiously, And found them a natural bench of rock set at a safe distance from the platform's drop. He let Gray have the first drink.

"Anyway, you did catch something on my rod. One of the best of the day." The family had shared the silver-brown pollack that night.

"Stupid bloody rocks." Gray said.

"Ach, Dad'll probably get you another one, and maybe this time a reel that doesn't click, next year. They're the best ones."

They had finished what And calculated in a weighing movement to be half the can, a natural end to their break.

Instead of clambering up onto the moor, And led them along a lower path that skirted the wall of the cliff, which began to rise in height above them. The sea swell was directly beneath them, with sharp skerries close in, exposed by the low tide.

They stumbled sometimes on the unfamiliar terrain and And said, "Lucky this ledge's wide or Andrew Urquhart *would* be taking a swim!"

Presently they came to a large fissure in the cliff, double-backing into the shadow of a cave.

"Can't go over it, can't go under it. Guess we'll just have to go into it."

Gray said nothing. He tutted again.

"Hey," And chivvied him, "Do you remember when we were little, we used to say hello to Echo, under the railway bridge? Echo! Echo!"

"Echo!" Gray mustered, thinking of Dad who'd introduced the tradition, and flattered at not being little anymore. "Echo!"

Echo replied in kind, dutifully.

The cave was narrow and not deep. It had a shallow roof but was more a gash than a tunnel. The path gave up in the jumble of rocks and the two boys picked their way around and across juts and little ridges until they were at the back of the short cave floor.

There were five or six empty wine bottles on the ground. On the walls there were just two inscriptions in different hands, GERS, splashed and dripped, and a smaller, more careful Stewart J.

"Do you think that's our Stewart Johnson?" Gray asked.

Stewart Johnson lived on their estate. Mum called him "a bad boy" but he was also "naughty but nice." When his name came up she smiled with a smile that wasn't sure it should be smiling.

"Knowing him, probably!" Stewart was a few years older than And, so he didn't really know him.

They drank the rest of the can. Andrew threw it down into the sea below.

The boys peed down into the swell and watched the surface froth with the impact. They aimed at the floating can, both hitting it easily. Soon, unbalanced and taking in water, it sank.

"Come on, let's get up on to the moor."

Graham followed his brother as they moved on along the path climbing past the cave, gradually leading them towards the moor. Above and ahead of them they could occasionally see the dips of the cliff top path they had left in their descent to the rock platform. Their own track changed in character from the dark rock it shared with the rock pools and skerries to the coarse turf of the rough pasture above them.

They were surprised to come across some sheep as the path

began to steepen but the novelty did not refresh Gray. He was weary, light-headed.

"I want to go back."

"We can't go back, the tide's rising."

"I'm tired."

"Come on, there's probably lobster fishermen beyond the headland. Maybe porpoises. Or," he added hopefully, "a submarine."

"How are ye gonny see a submarine, even if there is one?" Gray didn't even bother to ask what the difference was between a porpoise and a dolphin.

"Periscope. If you've got your wits about you."

Their father said "If you've got your wits about you" for something that might not be completely true but would be difficult for the boys to disprove. A dog camouflaged as a pavement, for instance.

They trudged on.

Presently, it occurred to Gray to say, "Dad's not going to be too pleased if I tell him about all that beer."

"Ach, it was only one can."

"Fine then, I'll just tell him."

"Fine by me."

"Right, I will."

The going was difficult now and they said nothing for a few minutes. They were out of breath.

Finally, And turned round.

"Clype!" he said.

"No Ah'm no!"

"Aye ye are."

"No Ah'm no!"

"Well don't grass me off then."

They climbed a little further.

Gray thought about the Catholics in Ireland and how they shot their own people in the knees, 'grasses'. There was no one in a wheelchair in his school (the Catholic children called it Protestant, but his headmaster said it was Universal). Yet Gray had seen a disabled girl being wheeled by her mother into St. Eileen's Primary . . .

Slowly, with resignation, he said, "All right, I won't."

The sea path joined its higher brother right at the headland and the boys stared out at the open sea.

There were no lobster boats, no porpoises, of course no submarine. The sea kept on with its weighty preoccupation.

A little further down the coast, perhaps half a mile from the shore was an island, almost symmetrical, treeless, between grey and green, empty.

Half way back along the cliff path, Gray asked, "Is a clype a kind of cleg?"

"I think so," And judged.

Midges meant nothing to them compared to that evil fly. Gray would come to remember holidays for their heartbeats of danger: a farmer's sprung twitching cockerel ambushing him from beneath the motor-caravan; just off the platform one evening, an enormous Lion's Mane jellyfish with its sinister cooked-rhubarb density; and the quiet cleg, as light as aluminium, more an injecting machine than a living creature.

Coming up from the rock-pools their father met them with a bucket full of mussels.

"Find any crabs?" Andrew said as Dad said, "Did you see the island?"

"Yes" they all said, in three variations.

"It's a military place, dating back to the War. They tested disease-bombs there on a herd of sheep. It worked like a dream, but at the last minute something made them think twice before loading the planes. They were going to bomb the continent."

The boys looked at each other, both disappointed they had not had this knowledge beforehand. It had just looked like a common or garden island.

"Is it safe now?"

"Oh no, it's still lethal to set foot on the place. Didn't you see the signs?"

"Dad! Thanks for telling us!"

Graham noticed that there weren't any crabs in the bucket.

"Didn't you find any crabs?" he said, repeating And's first question with a degree of precocious melancholy.

"I saw plenty, actually. Soft-shelled ones, too. But I didn't have the heart, in the end, to use them for bait. I think there's something human about a crab. Something to be said for seeing things sideways. I snapped them, though." He patted his camera-bag.

They walked on towards the beach and joined their mother.

"I drank the water instead of painting with it!" she said. "So it was back to the oils. And painting from memory – with a little invention thrown in!"

They all looked at the hasty painting.

Graham's lost turquoise rod with its cheap but cherished reel lay on a sketchy floor of sand. The fish he had caught on his brother's rod lay there, too, a cartoon, almost pleased to be a trophy. It was the first time they had seen their mother's art so deliberately slapdash, so comic, so reductive, so tenderly purposeful.

The island, of course, wasn't part of the scene but whenever he glanced at the picture – it hung now in Linda and Gray's hall – he thought of that day and the harmless looking island they had seen ahead of them.

"It's yours Gray, if you want it," his mother had said. "Still life with rod, fish and clicky reel."

12

MERMAID

GRAY PARKED THE yellow car, nimbly he thought, between two military-style family cars, their bumpers about the height of Jas's neck.

Jas had seen the engineered furniture of a play-park on her side of the road, on the other side of a tall fence, and suggested a detour to "the tanks and bees". The corral was fenced with chain-link against the motorway and also, as a pictogram indicated, against dogs.

Gray held open the heavy steel gate as Jas passed through and now they trod onto the inches-thick pieces of bark. The metal activity structures were surrounded by a plastic emulation of tarmac, a surface with give but hardly any bounce.

Jas climbed up onto the first contraption, a climbing frame in the shape, Gray judged, of an attack helicopter.

"I'm going to rescue a mermaid," Jas said, taking the aircraft to be for civil use, "and feed her an oldish goldfish and vegetarian ham."

"Aw, poor goldfish! Poor vegetarian pigs!"

Jas appeared to ignore him then laughed feebly. She understood Gray was joking but this laugh told him she hadn't understood the joke itself. He hadn't understood it either.

As she swung from the tail of the stiff helicopter she said, "Dad, are goldfish made of real gold?"

"I don't think so, but I don't know what they *are* made of."

"Catch me, then!" she said, crossly.

Jas's arms strained and she let go.

"That's *me* rescuing the mermaid!" he said, catching her not quite elegantly, hugging the bundle. "The only one I can see on these choppy seas."

His daughter gave the same uncertain half-laugh and said "Hanks", wriggling out of his arms.

The tank was next, another climbing frame but with a slide incorporated this time.

Gray had awarded his elder brother a small but enduring scar on his chin when they were little: Gray had been hurtling down the chute, his black school brogues a blunt instrument, and And had been clambering up. Gray remembered most the accumulating blood seeping through And's fingers as he held his hand to his chin on the brisk walk home. This made Gray regard play-parks a little nervously. At the same time, any visit to these planned landscapes reminded him of breezy shouts to his parents when he was little, "Just going down by the river, Mum", "Just off to the woods, Dad." Those territories were worry-free: after Andrews' accident only the play park required a special appeal.

"Oh, friction!" Jas said from the top of the slide. The stainless steel was a little wet and her clothes, absorbent, impeded descent. Even the toy tiger wouldn't move far: Jas put it in her pocket. Gray gently pushed her and then, when there was still resistance, dragged her bumpily down. It was all rather stop-start, the rhythm of a learner-driver kangaroo-hopping the instructor's car. Jas knew that this was 'friction', a one-word substitute for an explanation, but it served well enough.

The bee was a sit-on sculpture in black and yellow, mounted on a large sprung coil. It was rounded and child-safe, without even a sting.

They had to wait while another father almost smothered a much younger boy as he held him tightly in the sleeves of his puff-anorak, buzzing back and forwards. These two were the only other occupants of the enclosure and it dawned on Gray that the second domestic Jeep must be parked there for a reason unconnected to infant play. Shops, perhaps, were within trolley distance.

The man and boy exchanged their bee for another creature pinned to an industrial spring nearby. It was a black and white dog which Jas identified, without lowering her voice, as a border collie.

Again the protective padded arms, insurance against wobble and totter.

Gray and the man exchanged looks and a smile, then returned to their own shortened field of family vision, the radius now of a father's arm.

"Giddy-up!" Jas said and the bee was a horse.

They jumped over the high mesh fence on the motorway side, over the motorway itself, and onto the flat roofs of the business units on the other side.

"Back again, now!" Jas commanded.

The stripy horse made no move.

"Back again!"

No movement once more.

"I'm not afraid to whip you, you know!"

A snort, and something like a horse-ish whimper.

No movement.

"Right!"

A harsh lash with the invisible whip.

The horse moved off with a defiant neigh, bringing its rider safely back to the army paddock.

"I only whip you if you disobey," Jas lectured the novice bee-horse as she dismounted.

"Swings, Jas?"

They ran to the little row of swings, not wholly trusting the emptiness of the play-park. At home the swings were often occupied and there were times when they had to leave without having had a turn.

Each time Gray pushed her he felt the muscles of his arms do work.

"Higher, Dad! Dangerously high!"

"Is that dangerously high?"

"No!"

"Is that dangerously high?"

"No!"

"Is that dangerously high?"

"No!"

Gray begged to differ and missed a push.

With such adjustments they soared and cruised in the stratosphere. The clouds and the moon could be touched, but not the sun.

After ten minutes or so Jas was persuaded to land.

"Come on, back in the car. We've got things to do."

"I'm thirsty, and you said I could have a drink of milk."

Gray closed the heavy gate behind him. They set off on foot.

13

STAR-FRUIT

GRAY HAD BEEN right: there was a supermarket nearby. It was a large brown-brick building about the size of a business school. They had walked hand-in-hand up a short street and then in single file round a pathless roundabout, and there it was, next to a petrol station and a cash-point.

They walked across the busy car park towards the supermarket's source of bright yellow light. They had to pause momentarily for the doors to sense their weight. Yes, they had mass, and the broad sheets of glass retracted in mechanised welcome.

Jas went straight to the herd of nose-to-tail trolleys, but Gray called her back.

"Look, here's the café."

"Dad, he's perfectly normal," Jas whispered, as if in reply.

Gray saw a thin young man, face pasty, "peely-wally" Gray and And would have said to each other. He was parking his portly ShopMobility scooter near the café entrance. He clambered off, betraying weakness in his muscles, bone-core fatigue.

Jas saw this, too, now: "Oh," she said, and, as if to clear herself of any taint of prejudice, explained prissily "Because if he was just playing on that disability machine that would have been wrong." With a hint of regret, she added, "They are only for people-with-disabilities."

"That's right, 'that would have been wrong.' 'They are only for people with disabilities.' Now, would you like some milk?"

Normally they might joke about choosing elephant juice to drink, a fantasy beverage like that. Wave tea. But Jas had asked for plain milk back at the park and Gray wanted to stay close to her. He wanted to obey the rules, as he deduced them, within the registers of language she chose to generate. Maybe that was a phrase Linda had quoted to him, "Communicating in the language the child chooses to generate."

Jas didn't tolerate studied naivety in children's books or in people. Like Linda's, Jas's 'Way of No' was more powerful than her 'Way of Yes.'

Gray had moments in Jas's company when he felt simultaneously elderly and immature. In the same way, her age seemed to oscillate between infancy and who knows what teenage year, sentence to sentence. An irritated response to one of their once-shared eccentricities - "That's boring, Dad!" - or worse, a sigh of weary disapproval - "That's boring, Dad." - quickened his heartbeat, shortened his breath.

"It's not important, Graham," Linda had told him, seeing he was worried. "She's not lived long enough to understand the damage a sharp word can make, thrown properly. You're flattering yourself, thinking you're a deliberate target."

They sat down with their drinks. He'd chosen milk, too.

Their table and chairs were bolted to the floor at some distance from each other. Jas had to take care lifting the tub of milk to her lips.

They both found they were thirsty: they took great gulps but settled, before long, to sips.

Jas broke the silence: "There's a phone next to the toilets." She pointed.

Gray remembered himself. He had another look at his mobile, pressed its soft On button hard and long. His fingernail made a permanent little crescent in the rubber. Nothing.

He left the phone on the table and went into the toilets. There were bright yellow cubes of solid disinfectant in the urinals and he remembered when Jas, first seeing them on one of their early outings together, had cried out, "Sweeties!" She'd run to grab them, and Gray had had to shout.

When he got to the public phone the grey display flickered *Emergency only.*

He returned to the café.

Where was Jas?

Five minutes and where was Jas?

Just at the condiments stand.

She came back with some capsules of creamer and a pair of plastic stirrers. She added the creamer to her milk with some alacrity, vigorously stirring it with one of the tiny oars in each of her hands. A human blender, Gray thought.

"Do you want me to get you some? It's free, Dad."

"It's not really milk, you know. Or cream."

"It's free! Do you want me to get you some as well?"

"You don't have that stuff with milk!"

"It's fine! It's not delicious!"

"I don't want any."

"It's fine!"

"I'm fine!"

"Try some! They've got packets of sugar, too."

She spread a dozen or so packets of sugar across the table

and spilt a little opened creamer. A very white globule rested on Gray's silver mobile phone, which he noticed had been moved to Jas's side of the table.

Gray began to feel self-conscious, embarrassed.

The thin man looked across at them with a look that seemed to say, "A joke's a joke."

Gray also noticed a couple he had not noticed before. They were sitting together on a bench seat. They were wearing matching pink-and-white tops whose legends shared the single phrase between them: 'Neither One Thing . . .', 'Nor The Other.'

They looked in Gray's direction, and he thought they had the expression, "We both feel a bit let down by that sort of behaviour."

"You read too much into things," Linda would say to him, gently, whenever he worried aloud.

"It is a kind of intelligence," he'd once replied.

"Come on, Jas, finish up now."

Jas drank up. He picked up his phone, and they moved off. He noticed a surveillance camera swivel in their direction.

Gray thought they'd better think about a snack for car rations. He let Jas command a trolley and follow her gaze into the slopes of organised fruit. Red, green, yellow: he liked the idealism of the simple colours, internet-perfect. As an information professional he also had no faith in them.

"You read too much into everything," Linda would have said again. She'd have smiled with a smile they shared between them, just between them. Linda and Gray, Linda and Gray, Gray and Linda. She'd have bitten into a Golden Delicious, or a Cox's Pippin.

Star-fruit, Gray thought, as they moved out of the section.

Star-fruit, star-fish, and the human sign of a star: stylisation a way of being, the simplified life. He stretched his arms high and splayed his legs out. Jas didn't see him, he couldn't hold this pose for ever. He relaxed, caught up with her.

They found themselves among jams. Some of the jars had labels Gray had not seen since his childhood. Jas wanted to put a damson jar into her trolley but he wasn't in the mood for memory.

"There's bound to be a place for just sandwiches."

As he said this a fire alarm began to sound, in electronic pulses. Most shoppers stopped what they were doing and looked around to see what it meant. Gray did the same but took Jas's hand. After just a few seconds a woman's voice crackled, soared and swooped on a Tannoy.

"This is not a drill. This is not a drill. Will you please leave your shopping and go calmly to Assembly Point – to Assembly Point." She stopped and then appeared to find a text from which to read. "Will you please leave your shopping and go calmly to Assembly Point B positioned at the rear of the car park, where our fire marshals will meet you."

Gray and Jas followed the half-disgruntled, half-excited crowd out of one of the fire-exits. Some shoppers brought their trolleys with them and Gray hoped Jas wouldn't see there were free 3-D spectacles with the family packs of Coco-Pops. One lens red, one lens green: the representation of distance.

"Come on Jas, back to the car."

The roundabout was congested with cars exiting from the supermarket car park. Father and daughter walked easily within the standstill. Gray thought how the armour and technology of modern warfare was its greatest weakness, its own weight and sophistication so easily turned against itself: disabled, exploded or pointed back at its suddenly appalled directing powers.

They found their way back to the terrace of ex-shops they had passed on the way to the supermarket. Some windows were covered with a wash of white paint, but newspapers seemed the best concealers.

As the car park came into view Gray could see that one of the cars shielding the yellow car from view had gone. When they got closer Jas cried out, "Dad, we've got a stripe!" Gray could see that someone had taken a rock, or perhaps a key, and scratched a near-perfect line along one side.

"Interesting," he said, finding himself imitating his elder brother's methodical way of handling the unexpected. He should hardly be feeling emotional about damage to a car that many, he thought, might judge did not precisely belong to him. With this sense of annoyance, hidden with a borrowing from Andrew's reserve, he now had to recognise that he'd grown possessive about the little car.

"Maybe it's a go-faster stripe" he said, philosophically, "You know, like those on track-suits."

14

AN ARGUMENT

"THE ZOO DEFINITELY has a phone, Dad."

If they stayed on the motorway it would bring them close the long way round. Maybe that was easier than coming off. Linda would have found the first turn-off, anxious on the simple motorways, confident in the intricate urban capillaries. She'd almost be there by now.

All the lanes in both directions were slowing down, beginning to coagulate. On the other side they saw a police car and a military Land Rover parked at a distance from each other on the hard shoulder. In a glimpse Gray could see the two officers out on the red tarmac were arguing with each other. They were making apoplectic hand gestures while their respective drivers waited at the wheel.

Gray judged from their cars that they were middle-ranking officers. The backdrop was a field of rough pasture with a brown and white Shetland pony peeping through a wooden fence, exactly halfway between their vehicles.

Gray moved on with the traffic. More army lorries passed them on the other side. After fifteen minutes, suddenly that airport-bound lane was empty. They soon came to a junction and saw a police road-block had entirely sealed it off. The traffic was being channelled back on itself, one line out off the motorway altogether, one line feeding onto Gray's side. It was at walking speed or less.

Gray switched Ted off and the radio on. Silence. He pressed each favourites button, and it was the same. Not the fuzz of the spaces between radio stations: active silence. He used the scan button, and the radio located station after station, each without sound. Finally, he caught fragments, 'island', 'airport', a local voice, perhaps from the south of the city, and then it was silence for that station, too.

"Everyone's gone shopping!" Jasmine said and Graham smiled, laughed, once, almost a sneeze through his nose.

Now the traffic was moving only in stops and starts. Presently the reason for this became clear. A roadblock had been set up on this side, too.

Gray was not sure whether the military or the police had won the argument, but like the other roadblock this was staffed by police. Surely by chance, all the officers were women. This time they weren't diverting the traffic but, rather, speaking to each and every driver as the cars were funnelled through the checkpoint.

Gray found his Department pass. He was required always to carry it. It would give him access to most prohibited areas if he wanted.

They approached the checkpoint, window button-hummed down. A woman with a black and white riot helmet, surely too small for her, leaned into the car. A curved sheet of Perspex, the visor, was raised above her forehead, friendly setting. She smiled when she saw the same posture of enquiry from Gray, Jas, and the tiger in the child's hands, each looking her way.

"There's been a major industrial accident at the airport so we're having to redirect the other lane away."

"I've seen Army but no fire service. No helicopters, even. Is it something above the ordinary? Is it air-borne?"

She gave him a look which might have been surprise. It might have been recognition: of facts which until now she had not properly registered herself.

Gray regretted asking the question, it might help to identify him, and he decided not to show his pass. It was very unlikely she would have been briefed at such a level of detail. In fact, it would have been against all procedure. And he was, after all, in a bright yellow stolen car, a version of the tempting slot-machine rides placed just inside malls. They were a conspicuous couple, not your run-of-the-mill car thieves.

"It's just routine, sir. As routine as these things can be."

"We live near the Zoo. Can we get back there?"

"Dad!"

"That's a lovely place to live." The police officer was speaking to Jas. Gray thought of all that groomed parkland, the re-introduced red squirrels. "I bet your tiger feels at home there!"

The driver behind them beeped, "Hate to interrupt your conference."

The police officer acknowledged him with her hand.

"Dad!" Jas said again.

"It's those who live or work near the airport we're concerned about at the moment. When you get home, stay in and keep an eye on the television news." She said the full-length word 'television' as if it was unfamiliar to her when off duty. It was a term she would have been advised to use in court.

Before Gray could ask about the mute radio she moved

him on and they joined the queue of slow traffic. He wanted to ask about the island he had seen on the screens in the mall, the island he now realised, of course, was the forbidden island of his childhood.

15

DUNGEON TACTICS

THE ISLAND AND the airport: Graham couldn't understand the connection. There had been an outbreak of the disease in sheep on the mainland next to the island, before the war had come to an end. It had been controlled with slaughter, the farmers compensated with a financial hush and a veiled threat, the word 'treason' not quite having to be specified. An appeal for secrecy for the sake of national security had been added for good measure: there was a war on.

Another island further south, Gruinard, had been used as a testing ground for a variant of the disease, but that strain had been less troublesome.

It was also less cruel than its northerly sibling. Gruinard's pathogen, after an agony of days, did at least kill its victims. In the biology of the disease that had been earnestly seeded on Graham's childhood island, there wasn't a molecule of kindness.

It did begin its attack in the same way, via the respiratory system. The disease fastened itself to the soft tissue of the lungs. Graham wasn't the only Department official to wonder why 'controlled experiments' using air-borne organisms had been conducted in one of the windiest places in the British Isles: the Hebrides weren't known for their doldrumish calms, and these particular islands were within spitting distance, as it were, of the mainland. Gray imagined all kinds of strategic compromises had been made, with the usual measure of official idiocy and English nationalism thrown in.

Idiots – that was the generous word for what victims of the disease would become. More than half of any given sample, based on drily reported animal experiments Graham could still not forget, would not actually die. Instead, through a limited but critical period of oxygen deprivation, which appeared to be brought to a close by the pathogen moving on to the brain (a weaker, second-stage occupation), all victims became profoundly brain-damaged.

Perhaps, Gray imagined, just one official had managed, through the luck, say, of an authoritative personality – (he couldn't help seeing himself as an authoritative personality) – to persuade his head of department that the idea of a 'perfect revenge', the cold symmetry of vengeance, was precisely a Nazi concept, and so one that the British must avoid?

More likely, the clinching argument was the dawning fear that a capricious breeze could easily blow the spores back across Europe, back across the Channel.

Even Gruinard, where the less horrific strain had been tested, had only recently been declared safe, many decades after the experiment. Graham's predecessor had been involved in the sign-off.

Gray's island would never be signed off.

He tried to switch his phone on again. He hoped against hope that there'd be enough juice left for him to read any further messages from And.

Yes. One message had come in.

The phone rang before he could access it.

It was Linda, recorded on the voice-mail: "Have you heard? Can you give me a call anyway? If you've gone onto the Zoo can you just get indoors somewhere, anywhere. Not the lion enclosure!" She was worried, but she laughed. "They're not saying it's windblown, but it looks—. Anyway, *you* know what they're like: say one thing. Sorry about this morning by the way."

The phone's data turned itself away again, a blank screen. He'd have to wait before powering up and retrieving the text message.

Jas asked if it was Mummy on the phone.

(Her voice and Linda's voice, the way she briefly laughed in her message, the laughter that knew his face, smiling, would imagine her face, smiling – a particular look and a particular look. Even that as-if-casual 'by the way', just the sort of apology Linda would give. But it was an apology. And the way she guessed he'd take Jas somewhere special. Clairvoyance down to the bloody location!).

"Is it Mummy, Dad?" Jas said again, with a look he couldn't translate, perhaps guilt.

Yearn, he remembered from his student days, *out-dated word. Reason?*

"Uh-huh, but the batteries are dead again."

"Daddy, there really is a phone at the Zoo."

Six weeks after Linda's operation she had conceived Jasmine. Perhaps success after several years of infertility was down to whatever the material cause was beneath the statistical magic of that surgical procedure – the physio-psychology of the placebo effect, or an unrecognised but simply physical result of the key-hole invasion.

Gray thought differently.

He remembered staggering out of the bed, exhausted, laughing - grabbing Linda's ankles and hauling her upside down, holding her like that, a giggling willing torture victim strung up by her feet for the half a minute his strength could manage. And then his collapsing awkwardly into her arms.

"Just making sure you're getting every drop!" he muttered.

The last thing he remembered before falling into deep sleep was how they were joined to each other along almost the entire length of their bodies by the tender meniscus of their sweat. The joyous adhesion, the living congruence.

"Dungeon tactics," she'd called the legs up in the air business, smiling with that smile again, talking in bed.

Yearn. Out-dated word. Reason?

They drove on east, the traffic thinning as they came to each new junction. Strategically placed roadblocks saw that no new traffic was being allowed onto the motorway, and the traffic that remained moved, with the blessing of the police, with more ease.

On the lanes opposite, only the Army could be seen, moving quickly west. There was light artillery now and again and some military fire tenders but the bulk were covered trucks, presumably full of soldiers, and larger vehicles the size of removal lorries. Some transporters had clearly been commandeered and bore the lettering of a stage management firm, crowd barriers perhaps. These travelled in a single convoy of six, with an armed escort at the front and back of the line.

At one point Gray recognised forensic and decontamination Portakabins on a dozen low-loaders, hurtling by.

He thought again how they'd not seen a single aircraft all day; even, now he thought about it, as they had skirted the airport. Ground troops only: he imagined further soldiers and technical staff would have been summoned in strength from the south and west. Air power would mean nothing against the island disease, helicopters would churn the air. The infantry was needed to seal the area off, but no one could seal a breeze.

After all his years of training, his routine but, he thought, real devotion to the Department, he was surprised to feel a tremendous sense of relief. His public service commitment was to the noble but abstract concept of the protection of the people (he believed, not without a mixture of pride and resentment, Scotland was a nursery for servants of the British state). But whatever the catastrophe was it had happened on somebody else's watch. Blue Shift wouldn't phone him – they had their hands full. If it was 'procedurally incorrect' who would point a finger at such a time?

And he was colluding with the silence. He was not going to contact them now: a husband who wasn't sure if he was leaving his wife, a father who wasn't sure if he was kidnapping his own child. A civil servant who was absolutely certain he had stolen this infantile canary-yellow car.

If there was one thing he did well, Gray was thinking, it was cowardice. Yellow was just the right colour. Even dramatising himself as a deserter was a dodge: regard the heroism of the anti-hero.

He glanced across at Jas and she smiled back. She seemed to have aged months, years, this journey. Not the only one, he thought to himself, with a cartoon roll of the eyes.

Linda and Gray, Gray and Linda. They took each other for granted. They had to take each other for granted. You couldn't be super-conscious of each other all your lives, could you? Their jobs, Jas, who did what around the house: you'd made this pattern together and you each moved within the pattern.

It began as improvised, but it was now almost fixed: you couldn't have one of you making up brand new flourishes, twisting, obscuring the original shape of things. Could you?

Could you, could you, could you?

Linda and Gray, Gray and Linda.

Linda and Gray and Jas, Jas and Gray and Linda.

Gray, Gray, Gray.

"Just because I don't need nappies doesn't mean I don't need to go to the toilet!"

Gray noted to himself the sophisticated sentence construction, the rhetorical power of the three negatives: she really was brighter than she had been this morning.

They stopped briefly on the hard shoulder. Jas was self-conscious as the traffic sped by and wouldn't go near the scrubby verge. She faced into the front wheel and decorated the alloy hub-cap.

Gray tutted but not passionately. He remembered the homicidal driver and his silver ear-clip. He felt proprietorial, then mildly self-righteous; then he felt sheepish and then he felt amused.

Soon after, they re-joined the traffic. A little later their exit finally came up.

Gray touched the twig of the indicator. With a satisfying click-click click-click (why did companies bother to make a fishing reel that *didn't* click?) they left the motorway.

16

PENDING FATHER INVESTIGATION

"AWAY AND RECYCLE yourself, then!" Linda had shouted at him this morning. It was the first time she had ever shouted at him. He had slammed the door and that was a first, too.

He had heard his mother's seashore painting fall from the wall.

"You could say today was a day of firsts," he thought to himself. In fact, he wasn't sure if he had actually mumbled "A day of firsts," out loud.

No, Jas was undisturbed. They were driving along a grey high street with the road separated from the shops by unbroken steel railings at the pavement edge.

Linda was right. He had wanted to shout at himself, too. And at everyone and everything else, every animate thing, every inanimate thing, what was the difference.

A few weeks ago, he had showed her the official letter with its misspelling, 'suspended pending father investigation'.

He had laughed and Linda had not laughed.

She did not value words in the same way.

Of course, work would never have contacted him today: suspended is suspended.

Rightly suspended.

You don't dig away at Her Majesty's Government's experiments on the personal territories of your childhood and evade capture. You don't pull out memos and reports to grow your little dossier and escape Scot free.

And the result: thousands of words to fill the simple blank of an island he had not remembered well enough to recognise on the rows and rows of TVs today.

Recycle yourself. Investigate farther. Suspension.

He felt he had been in suspension for years, closed to himself and closed to everyone else.

17

THE ZOO

GRAHAM PARKED THE car in a fountain, and they got out Jasmine's side to keep their shoes and socks dry.

"Can we check to see if Looby Loo is in the boot?"

"We're in a bit of a hurry, now. We're nearly at the Zoo."

The park was busy. They'd had to drive through quickly moving crowds of families, all not quite walking and not quite running over the grass. The adults had seemed flustered rather than outraged, as if it was all quite understandable, really, but did that man have to drive that car here and now, through us?

Most of the children seemed uncharacteristically biddable for modern children, not pulled along like sheet-anchors by brow-furrowed parents. They moved energetically with them. Their faces were as openly but shallowly concerned as if they were living photocopies of the faces of their elders.

He stopped one mother and daughter. They were moving so fluently in time with each other he thought of them as champion oddballs competing together in a choreographed three-legged race, no participating couple allowed the luxury of physical ties.

"What's the panic?

"We've all been told to go home and stay at home. Keep

doors and windows shut. Chimneys blocked. As if anyone has chimneys these days."

"Why? Who told you?"

"The Zoo, the Government. The Government's telling everyone. It's real, but that's all anyone knows."

She gripped her daughter again and they moved off, quickly resuming the synchronised movements of their dance.

Graham held Jas's hand, and they picked their way through and against the throng, Graham urging her on with his quickened pace. Jas seemed happy to be rushed along. Maybe they were dancers, too – or dodging through the oncoming crowd was a new game and they were winning it together.

The last fifty metres before the entrance were easier going. Gray inferred that the Zoo was now simply empty. They rushed up to the only ticket booth still open.

"What on earth is going on?" he asked the window.

"No one's switched the light on for me, either," said a young woman with an Australian accent, emerging from Gray's reflection. "I've been in this cage all day? We were told just half an hour ago to get everyone out and that's what we're doing? When I get the OK I'm out of here, too?"

"Is the shop still open?" Graham asked, attracted to the questioning cadence. He was sorry to reply with a real enquiry. Her apparent humility in the face of her own eye-witness testimony made him feel protective, or at least desire to touch her.

She had one hand next to the window, holding a pen with a sentinel Meerkat top. He placed his left hand on the steel counter, which felt cool.

Gray recognised his thoughts as far from paternal. He was alive and if she was alive – to him – this surge would be forgiven.

Her dark hair and eyes suggested Italian parents, perhaps.

He smiled and made eye contact.

She did not smile. She broke eye contact and withdrew her hand. She asked an aggressive question.

"Haven't you got the picture, yet? No one's getting in. Any minute the taxis will be arriving for the penguins."

Gray was not able to decide if the ticket box sentry was joking. She seemed poised between a particularly dry tone of irony and an indignant defence of the Zoo's due diligence. He was sorry that the tone of self-doubt had stopped, at exactly the same time, he noticed, when real doubts entered the semantic field of her statements.

Jas looked at Graham with a look of annoyance. She was not partial to the absurd.

Perhaps, Gray thought, she saw his attraction to the stranger.

He remembered himself.

With his right hand he placed his lottery ticket on the counter, a decoy. He climbed quickly but awkwardly over the turnstile's stiff chrome loop.

Jas already had her arms reaching up to him. He lifted her over it. He didn't remember these barriers from his last trip. Fraud or foxes?

They ran in the direction of the ape cages as they heard the woman shout behind her.

"Hey, how do you know my numbers!"

As they ran, Jas skipped by leading on the left then leading on the right, mastered without practice in a day.

All the apes were on holiday or in their hidden homes, watching commercials for tea perhaps.

"Is the pig with a moustache still alive?
"We're just going to the shop, remember."
"I want to see the pig with the moustache."
"We're not seeing the pigs with the moustaches."
"She might have died since last time."
"They won't have died since last time. Now listen, the whole point of coming here is to buy a lion."
"I don't want a stupid lion. I hate lions. I want to see the pigs."
"It's either the lion or nothing."
"I. Want to see. The pigs. With the MOUSTACHES."
"Right, you can jolly well just go back home and see how you like that!"
Gray gripped Jas's wrist and started to pull her back towards the entrance.
He wanted his voice to have natural authority, but he sounded too high-pitched.
Jolly well?
Threatless.
She punched him with her free hand in the stomach.
He sought to bring her under control, picking her up and holding her close to his chest. She bit him through his sweat-shirt, just below the shoulder.
"Fine!" he shouted, still too shrill, almost hitting her, blushing as if the deserted Zoo was full of people. "If that's the way you want to play it, home we go."
He moved further back with her, but Jas burst into tears, her body becoming limp and somehow heavier, harder to carry. Gray had to put her gently on the ground.
"You're the worst Dad there is! I hate you. I don't even love you." She had her face on the dusty tarmac. She was sobbing.

This was the crying that Gray recognised as deep crying, crying beyond the tears she seemed able to turn on and off. This sobbing had the momentum of injustice and then the momentum of sobbing itself.

He had learned to be impervious to shallow tears but not to these. This day, these days, everything. He was about to sob himself.

"Crying will save us. It's the end of the world."

An athletic man in sporting Lycra, black, lime and violet, was suddenly close, talking to them softly. His nearly yellow hair was well-groomed and he smelt of teenage after-shave.

Gray took a second to recover as Jas flinched and staggered to her feet. He straightened up and with a touch on her shoulder moved her away, behind him.

"Christ and the Prophet, peace be upon Him, told us and we wouldn't listen. We have to be the new Noahs, now." The man wasn't preaching; he was talking as if they had known each other for years. Here they were, discussing the recent weather, a little dull of late.

"So, where's your snorkel, pal?" Gray said, finding and exaggerating a Glaswegian accent. "How about having a recce for it in the piranha tank." He was surprised at his own aggression but not ashamed of it.

Three mustard-coloured monkeys ran past them, stopped, looked up at them, then ran on.

"It's our fault, friend."

The man briefly placed his hand on Gray's arm who pushed him away.

"Join me in prayers, here with the great apes, our witnesses."

Gray and Jas glanced in at the cage, but the gorillas were still indoors, out of sight.

The man placed a white tea-towel, printed with dark Celtique latticework, onto the ground. He knelt down and asked them again to pray with him.

"Not big enough to share, really, is it?" Gray said, scooping Jas up and walking away.

A light brown plated animal, the size of a heavy spaniel, trotted past them like a remote-controlled toy, half miniature personnel carrier, half oversize pine-cone.

Jas and Gray looked at each other and smiled.

"Is that an armadillo?" she asked him.

"Not precisely, but it's the same sort of thing." Educational, this trip. "It's a mandolin. I mean a pangolin."

"Eats ants?"

"Eats ants."

They were walking quickly now, getting away from the athletic religionist, synchronising with the sense of hurry they'd seen in the animals.

They reached the shop. It was abandoned like the rest of the zoo. One door next to a coin-operated tiger was ajar. They walked in and Jas said, "Dad, can I have this?"

It was a large snowy owl, a soft toy.

"Just a plastic lion."

"It doesn't cost much." There was no price on it. Jas couldn't understand prices.

"Just a plastic lion."

He moved on to give the impression of the owl being out of the question, dealt with. Jas picked up the owl and followed him.

"Jas."

"Dad."

"Jas."

"Dad."

"Jas."

"Mum would buy me this."

"Uh-huh."

"She would."

"Is that right."

"She cares about me."

"I'm sure she does."

"You—"

"Yes?"

"You're hurting my feelings. We mustn't hurt each other's feelings. It could damage us for life." Jas looked up and saw Gray's raised eyebrows. He recognised the words of Jas's teacher, oddly keen to give children articulate psychological reasons for their bad behaviour. His experience was that this merely strengthened their arsenal of manipulative weaponry.

Jas put the owl down, on a shelf of floppy books about amphibians.

They found the plastic lions and Jas picked one.

The till was shut down but Gray made a point of leaving some loose change next to the key-fobs.

Outside, the square was a troubled crossroads of animals and large flightless birds. They were worried and even fractious, but the predators were not hunting.

Kangaroos, a water buffalo and a hefty pigmy hippo bumbled together, wrong-footing each other as smaller animals scurried around them. Briefly kiwis, emus, and ostriches came together as if the continents had resolved themselves into a single land mass again. For a second skunks, penguins and a pair of wild magpies all faced each other in black-and-white amazement before scattering their separate ways.

Gray and Jas skirted round the square, their way to the exit cut off by the mass of animals. Several hyenas guarded a phone booth with their sneers. Gray remembered, a little late, that he should call work, Linda, his brother.

A lion some way off stood its ground against the creature rush-hour. It managed to roar casually, as if yawning, an unmoved authority amidst the growing panic of the other animals.

Gray could feel his breath getting shorter.

"Think my allergy's acting up, Jas."

"But I thought it was just cats, dogs, horses, sheep, and goats."

"Think it must be animals in general. Let's just get, get to somewhere quieter."

They walked down a shrub-lined path which ended at an enclosure surrounded by own a short fence. Gray was now clutching his chest and labouring to carry the bag.

"She hasn't died, Dad! Look!"

On the other side of a moat, facing them, not quite looking at them, was a large pig with a moustache.

Something moved at the side of his vision as Gray looked on. He turned his head and saw the lion walking towards them and stopping perhaps fifteen metres away. It yawned/roared again, and Gray flinched.

"OK, just let's get over this fence here." Gray said, lifting her over ahead of him. His voice was thick now, underpowered, he could feel his lungs tense, their air-capacity lessening. Please be a simple allergy.

He followed his daughter, deliberately slowing himself down so he'd appear calm to lion and Jas both.

"OK, love, up!" He held her as high as he could but

still close to him and they entered the moat together.

The water came up to his navel, submerging his wallet and his mobile phone.

It was not easy to get out and Gray had to move a little further along to find a shallower bank on the other side. Up on dryish ground, a glance back and the lion had moved on.

The pig with the moustache had retreated to its family at the other side of the enclosure. Several of the animals were looking their way.

Gray took his trousers off and set them across one of a group of vast logs. He was shivering. Perhaps they would be dry by the end of the day, but it wouldn't be long before light started to fail. He kept his knickers on, though they were soaked, too.

"I think we'll just have to stay on this island for a little while. Until we hear it's safe to go back home."

It hurt his chest to speak.

Jas looked pale and he cuddled her in towards him, finding her little warmer than he was.

"Dad, this is the best day we've ever had," she said, beginning to cry again.

This book has been typeset by
SALT PUBLISHING LIMITED
using Neacademia, a font designed by Sergei Egorov for the Rosetta Type Foundry in Czechia. It has been manufactured using Holmen Book Cream 65gsm paper, and printed and bound by Clays Limited in Bungay, Suffolk, Great Britain.

CROMER
GREAT BRITAIN
MMXXVI